Sunshine And Rain

Book 9

Rain Series

Sunshine

And Rain

Vanessa
Miller

Book 9
Rain Series

Other Books by Vanessa Miller

Sunshine and Rain (rel. Oct. 29, 2016)
Family Business Book III (Love & Honor)
Family Business Book II (Sword of Division)
Family Business Book I
Rain in the Promised Land
After the Rain
How Sweet The Sound
Heirs of Rebellion
Heaven Sent
Feels Like Heaven
Heaven on Earth
The Best of All
Better for Us
Her Good Thing
Long Time Coming
A Promise of Forever Love
A Love for Tomorrow
Yesterday's Promise
Forgotten
Forgiven
Forsaken

Rain for Christmas (Novella)

Through the Storm

Rain Storm

Latter Rain

Abundant Rain

Former Rain

Anthologies (Editor)

Keeping the Faith

Have A Little Faith

This Far by Faith

EBOOKS

Love Isn't Enough

A Mighty Love

The Blessed One (Blessed and Highly Favored series)

The Wild One (Blessed and Highly Favored Series)

The Preacher's Choice (Blessed and Highly Favored Series)

The Politician's Wife (Blessed and Highly Favored Series)

The Playboy's Redemption (Blessed and Highly Favored Series)

Tears Fall at Night (Praise Him Anyhow Series)

Joy Comes in the Morning (Praise Him Anyhow Series)

A Forever Kind of Love (Praise Him Anyhow Series)

Ramsey's Praise (Praise Him Anyhow Series)

Escape to Love (Praise Him Anyhow Series)

Praise For Christmas (Praise Him Anyhow Series)

His Love Walk (Praise Him Anyhow Series)

Could This Be Love (Praise Him Anyhow Series)

Song of Praise (Praise Him Anyhow Series)

1

Isaac Judah Walker rolled out of bed drenched in sweat. He was having that dream again. The one where God showed him things that he did not want to see, hear or even know about. As he got out of bed and jumped into the shower, trying to shake the feeling that he was supposed to be doing something about his dream. He didn't have time to get involved with anything other than what he was currently doing, so he wished that God would stop invading his sleep.

His father told him that being able to see into the supernatural was supposed to be some kind of gift. If that was true, he wanted to return that gift to the sender.

"You want company in there," Alexa his live in girlfriend asked as she opened the shower door.

She looked so seductive in that short nighty, that he almost invited her in. But he didn't have time for any delays this morning. There was too much on the line. "I'm just getting out." He turned off the water and wrapped a towel around himself.

"Your loss," she said as she took out a tooth brush and started brushing her teeth.

"I've got an important meeting, but I'll make it up to you by taking you some place nice later on tonight."

She spit the tooth paste out, and rinsed out her mouth. "Sounds good. I'll make the reservations."

He quickly dressed and headed out of the house. He hadn't even stop to kiss Alexa goodbye. As he jumped into his two-seater convertible his cell phone rang. "Speak," he said, using his hands-free car phone.

"Boy, I know I raised you with better manners than that," Nina Walker yelled into the phone.

"Sorry about that, Mama. I have a lot on my mind, so I wasn't paying attention when I answered the phone… didn't know it was you."

"What difference does that make? Do you really think that answering the phone like that is the right thing to do, Judah?"

Years ago his mother and the rest of the family called him Ikee. After college he was able to convince them that he was a full grown man who should be called by a grown man name. Instead of using his first name, which belonged to his father, the dynamic Pastor Isaac Walker, he decided to use his middle name. Now everyone referred to him as Jude, which was short for Judah. He had his mother to thank for the fact that his middle name meant praise, but Jude wasn't giving out much praise to the Lord these days. Which is the reason he went by the shortened version of his middle name. But his mother refused to shorten it. "I'll do better, Mother. Now what can I do for you. I have back to back meetings this morning so I can't stay on the phone long."

"Not planning to keep you long. I just want to know if you'll be home for Thanksgiving or Christmas this year."

Frustration edged the tone of each word, "This is the end of August. How am I supposed to know what I'll be doing in a few months?"

"You haven't been home in three years, Judah. I know you work hard and your building a career, but family is important too."

"True that… look, all I can say is that I'll try my best to get away from work this year. Okay."

"I guess I'll have to take that and add a bit of prayer to it," Nina told her son as they hung up the phone.

Jude pulled his car into the executive parking spot. He turned off the engine and just sat there a moment. Life had been so much simpler when he was a kid and believed like his parents. But the education he received at college and the years he'd been away from home had caused him to question the 'just believe' mantra Christians crammed down the throats of non-believers.

What was the use anyway, preachers keep preaching and sinners keep sinning. And the real sad part was that preachers were doing just as much sinning as the congregation. But Jude didn't have a negative opinion of all pastors like a lot of his friends. Because Jude had been raised by Isaac Walker a man who loved God, his family and the church. The man he was named after, even though his mom had slipped Judah in as his middle name, Isaac Walker was a man after God's own heart. Jude had much respect for his father and for preachers because of the man who raised him. But at this point in his life he was just trying to do him, and to make as much money as he possibly could, while he was still young enough to enjoy it.

Right out of college he and two friends had a great idea for an online commerce business, but no money to purchase the product. His father had loaned them the money and it had been full speed ahead ever since. But now they were dealing with growing pains, and his partners thought selling the company was the best thing for all. Jude had put blood sweat and tears into this company and didn't want to let it go. The meeting this morning would determine if he had persuaded one of his partners over to his side of the fence.

Micah Davenport was already seated in the conference room when Jude arrived, which didn't surprise him. Micah was always the early bird. Stephen Johnson their third partner often had no regard for other people's time. Glancing at his watch, Jude asked, "Have you heard from Stephen?"

Micah shook his head. "Not since last night. But he's the one who called this meeting, so I'm sure he'll be here shortly."

Jude sat down across from Micah and gave his friend and business partner an awkward smile. During his senior year in college Jude, Micah and Stephen had been inseparable. They had stumbled on to developing an app that helped the average person study the Bible. But the more they worked on the app, the more Jude and Micah allowed Stephen to expand the idea so that it was no longer just for studying the Bible, but it also became a study guide for history, science and economics. Their app became all the rage for college kids looking for a quick and easy way to pass tests without actually reading their books chapter by chapter.

Even though the three of them started their app with the same purpose in mind, they were nothing alike. Micah was white, but had lived just one step up from a trailer on the poor side of town. The only thing Micah had going for him was his 4.0 GPA. That 4.0 had earned him a scholarship and a way out of a life he wanted nothing to do with.

Stephen was the dark skinned brother that the ladies went wild over. He grew up in the Midwest where his father worked for the post office and his mother was a school teacher. Stephen detested everything about the Midwest, and about the modest twenty-five hundred square foot home and nice middle class neighborhood he grew up in. He liked fast cars and fast women. So he needed lots of money. Which was the reason Stephen wanted to enlarge their market pool by offering more than just a bible app.

Jude should have been the biggest and best advocate for keeping the bible app pure because he'd grown up in a Christian home. He'd seen first-hand how the preached word of God could bring about a revival. But he too had been seduced by the money that could be made by expanding the idea.

"Look Micah, I really don't understand why you want to force this sale. We're doing good… making money." Jude just didn't understand why his old college buddy suddenly wanted nothing more to do with a business that had made him rich. Maybe he was getting greedy and needed to be as rich as God before he was satisfied.

Shaking his head, Micah told him. "I'm not letting you take the easy road on this one. You know why I want out. You just can't admit it or you'd have to call yourself a sellout."

"I'm a sellout because I like making money?"

"No, you're a sellout because you've never stood up for the original principals behind *Find It*."

Find It was the name of the app they developed. Jude had come up with the idea as he was leading a bible study group during college, and kids had so many questions that Jude started talking about the need for an app. Micah, who had been attending the bible study told Jude that he could make the app. So, Jude and Micah started working on it. Then Stephen, Jude's roommate at the time, convinced them that they needed a pitchman in order to sell the app, and the three-way partnership was born.

"I don't get why you're so ticked off about everything."

Micah stood up. He started to walk out of the conference room, but he then hesitated and turned back to Jude with sadness in his eyes. "When I attended your first bible study I was searching for something real, something that I could believe in. I gave my life to the Lord because of those bible studies."

"I know that, Micah. What I don't know is why you are tearing down everything that we've built."

"Because I will not be a part of a company that promotes cheating. Stephen wants me to create apps that provide test answers. I have no idea how I would do that, but even if I could, the whole idea goes against my faith and belief system."

"When Stephen gets here, we can talk to him about that. Let's just tell him that our company isn't going in that direction." Jude tried to reason with Micah.

But Micah wasn't having it. "You should have told him that when he took our focus off of creating an app to answer bible questions. But we all had dollar signs in our eyes. I'm just thankful to God that money no longer defines me."

Jude laughed out loud. "Easy to say now that you're rich. And the sale of the company would only make you richer."

"Look, I'm tired of arguing with you and Stephen over this matter… Buy me out, then we won't have to sell the company."

"You know we can't afford to buy you out."

"Then we have nothing else to talk about."

"Sit back down, Micah. This company has made you a millionaire. So, the least you can do is hear me and Stephen out before making any final decision."

Micah sighed. He pulled out the chair and sat back down.

Jude glanced at his watch. Stephen was late most of the time, but he normally ran in a minute or two after the meeting began. They'd been sitting in the conference room for almost twenty minutes, but hadn't heard a word from Stephen.

Jude took out his cell phone and started to call Stephen. But at the same time, the conference door opened. His administrative assistant, Tyra Malcom walked in. Tears were streaming down her face as she tried to wipe them away with the balled up tissue in her hand.

Jude put his cell down as he stood and rushed to her. "What's wrong, Tyra? Why are you crying like this?"

"I-it's Stephen. He's dead."

Micah jumped out of his seat as Jude said, "What do you mean? What happened? Did he get into a car accident on the way to work?"

Tyra violently shook her head. "The police shot him."

2

For a long time after those words had been uttered, nothing seemed real. How could it be true that marketing genius, Stephen Johnson, had been shot dead during a routine traffic stop? But it was true, and the trigger happy cop who'd killed an unarm man as he tried to unstrap his seat belt hadn't been arrested. The only punishment that cop received was a three month suspension with pay.

Jude just wasn't sure how he felt about that. He wasn't sure how he felt about much of anything lately. He had lost a friend and a business partner, never mind the havoc some of Stephen's ideas were wreaking throughout the company. Jude wouldn't have wanted Stephen dead just so the business wouldn't be sold off and neither did Micah. He and Micah mourned every day for Stephen's loss, and they even commissioned a six foot painting and put it on the first wall visitors saw as they entered the building.

Stephen died without a will, because most twenty-eight year old men don't believe they need one. Even so, Jude and Micah opened the books and allowed Stephen's parents to understand what the company was worth and the amount they would be paying out to them. But Jude still didn't think they had done enough to honor Stephen's life and death. He walked around in sadness because he couldn't figure out what else he should be doing.

"Why are you still moping around here with your dusty old house coat on?" Alexa asked as she entered the kitchen.

Jude looked down at the robe his mother had given him three Christmases ago. The robe was earth tones with green, brown and tans swirled around like little tad poles. "My robe isn't dirty."

"Okay, the robe isn't dusty, but you look dusty because you've been in that thing since yesterday."

"What do you want from me, Alexa? It's Sunday. Can't I sit around my house in my robe on the weekend if that's what I choose to do?"

"We were supposed to go out to brunch this morning, or did you forget about our date again?"

"Don't put your hands on your hip and shake your head at me woman." Jude had been dating Alexa for two years now. She was a hot tempered, exotic beauty from south of the border. They met at a business expo Jude, Stephen and Micah had attended in order to market the updated version of their app. But as far as Jude had been concerned Alexa was the main event.

She was coming down a runway modeling a sea green off the shoulder mid length dress that took Jude's breath away. He had to have her, and since he had been nursing a broken heart for a year, and was getting tired of being alone, Jude made his move.

He'd pursued Alexa for a month before she went out on a date with him. Six months later she moved into his house and he hadn't been able to get rid of her since. Which would be a good thing if Jude was still infatuated with her, but the luster of their relationship wore off after about a year of living together. Partly because his family vehemently disagreed with his decision to shack up, and partly because he and Alexa had nothing in common. He liked football and basketball, Alexa thought that sports were silly. Jude was an early riser, believing as his mother used to say, 'the early bird gets the worm', while Alexa didn't get up before noon. Which was the reason she wanted to do brunch instead of breakfast.

"I'm going to do more than shake my head. I'm getting tired of just hanging around this house doing nothing. I want to party and you've declined every party we've been invited to in the last few months."

"I didn't turn down the invitation for you. Nothing stopped you from going to those parties."

"I'm glad you said that because there's a party tonight that I really want to attend."

Jude nodded. "Then go."

Alexa smiled gleefully as she kissed Jude on the cheek. "You mean it? You're okay with me going out tonight?"

He didn't respond because in truth, her excitement over going off to some party was another thing that didn't sit well with Jude. He wasn't a party animal and never had been. Growing up it was more about church than hanging out. During college he spent his spare time heading a bible study group and now that he had money and time to do whatever he wanted, partying still wasn't on his list.

Jude made himself a bowl of cereal, plopped down on the sofa and picked up the remote. It was Sunday so there was sure to be a Law & Order marathon on some channel. He'd watch Law & Order until the game he wanted to see came on.

Alexa stomped her foot. "You're really just going to sit there watching TV?"

"You could help. I need snacks for the game."

"Football!" she screamed. "You expect me to sit around here waiting on you hand and foot while you watch football?"

Lifting an eyebrow at Alexa's mini temper tantrum, Jude said, "So no snacks then?" He knew he was being a jerk, but didn't actually care. If Alexa couldn't enjoy the day just hanging out with him, doing something he wanted for a change then she could do whatever she wanted to do and leave him in peace.

She turned in a huff and stormed out of the room. "I don't have to put up with this, Jude. I have plenty of friends who don't mind spending the day being adventurous and having fun."

Jude turned the volume up as he put Alexa out his mind, drifted back to a time when he'd found love that he thought would last a lifetime. Marissa Allen had been a sweet girl, who'd gotten herself mixed up with some bad people. But one day Jude had knocked on her door and invited her to the revival that his father was doing in the inner city.

Marissa had attended the revival, and she and Jude had become inseparable afterwards. He thought he would marry Marissa. But when he came back for her after graduating from college and starting his business, Marissa had questioned his commitment to God and the work of the ministry.

He couldn't believe that a girl who wouldn't have a relationship with God at all if he hadn't knocked on her door and implored her to come out to hear his father preach, was now looking down on him. He had gone off to college and educated himself just as everyone wanted. He'd even started a prosperous business, but none of that mattered to Marissa or his family either, for that matter.

His mother was always asking him to come home for a visit, but none of them realized how much they were judging his life choices… and the worst of all, the girl he fell in love with wanted nothing to do with him.

"Hopefully, you'll put some clothes on and be ready to go out into the world and experience life when I get back," Alexa told him as she slung her purse on her shoulder and headed out the door.

Jude put his bowl on the table and then stretched out on the sofa. He felt a little guilty for lounging around on a Sunday afternoon when he hadn't even attended church this morning. But he'd been missing church a lot these last few years.

After Stephen's death Jude began wondering if Stephen had enough time to get right with God before he drifted into that everlasting sleep. But then again, Jude wondered if there was sleep or rest for those who did not die in Christ. He wanted to call and ask his dad about some of the things that had been on his mind lately. But he couldn't bring himself to admit that he had doubts about the very thing he'd been raised on.

He felt a headache coming on, so he closed his eyes and tried to shut out the thoughts that had been bombarding his mind for months. He drifted off to sleep, hoping that peace would somehow overtake him.

But just as he was almost to "LaLa Land", Jude felt himself being pulled and yanked, and with great dread, he knew what would come next. His father had told him all about his trips to Hell. Jude had been fascinated by the whole ordeal, but about two year ago, the same things started happening to him, Now, Jude wasn't so much fascinated as he was terrified.

~~~~

No church service today, Isaac Walker had declared it 'give-back' day. This was the one day of the year that the congregation came to church, not to hear a sermon, but to be a sermon.

All the chairs and pews had been removed from the sanctuary and the room had been lined with one ten foot table after the next. hundred pound bags of rice, veggie grain mix and grains of barley lined the floor in front of the pulpit area. The saints of God positioned themselves at the tables and began filling small bags full of the different types of grain.

It was like an assembly line… one person packed the rice, veggie mix or barley in bags, while another put the bags on the scale to determine the exact weight. Once the grain in the bags met the measurement requirements, the bag was handed off to another saint who then sealed it. The sealed bags were then loaded onto a truck to be taken to the airport and delivered to Haiti in order to help with Hurricane relief… ministry.

Nina, Iona and Cynda helped out by filling containers with grains and then handing them over to the saints on the assembly line so they could fill the bags. While Isaac, Donavan and Keith helped load the heavy containers onto the truck.

"This is God's work, my boy," Isaac told Donavan as he patted his son on the back.

"That's what you told me three hours ago, before my back started aching like crazy." Donavan wasn't the only one doing a lot of heavy lifting. The brothers of the church had lined up outside and were passing the buckets from one man's muscle bound arms to the next. It was a powerful thing to see men and women working towards the common goal of helping less fortunate people. Haiti had just suffered another earth shattering hurricane. They were in desperate need of so many things. And the church had responded.

Donavan had been scheduled to preach this Sunday as he had the last few Sundays, because Isaac's aches and pains were showing up in more places and more frequently now that he was a think-he's-young, and good looking 85 year old man. But upon hearing of the devastation in Haiti, Isaac decided that the sermon could wait so they could take care of ministry.

Keith put a hand on Donavan's shoulder. "Me and your daddy was nothing but a bunch of takers when we was younger, so it does our heart good to give back these days." Keith lifted a hand to heaven. "God is so good for allowing us to still be around to be a blessing to someone else."

"That's the only reason we're still on earth... to be a blessing to others," Isaac told his son.

"You're right, Dad. And you had a good idea. The saints are working hard and loving every minute of it.

And we will be feeding hundreds of thousands of people."

"And what's also important," Keith told them as they headed back into the church to get the next buckets ready to load, "is that the saints have the opportunity to help others. They can now see how blessed their lives are in the good old US of A. Hopefully, they'll stop complaining and get on about the Lord's business. Because time is winding down."

Isaac grabbed hold of his arm, felt a bit dizzy but he kept walking. Nina met them at the door. She kissed her husband. "A hundred thousand, down and a hundred thousand more grain packs to go."

"Don't remind us," Donavan said.

Keith shoved Donavan. "Don't complain, young buck. While you still have the strength to do this kind of work you need to get in as much as you can. Might actually put some muscles on them skinny arms of yours."

"Whatever." Donavan flexed his muscles as he said, "Ain't nothing skinny about my arms. And my wife loves it."

"Boy, don't nobody want to see them little hills when my husband has mountains." Nina nudged Isaac. "Ain't that right, baby? Show your son what you're working with."

Isaac slightly turned to his right, getting ready to do exactly as Nina requested when a pain struck him so hard in the chest that he immediately grabbed for it. He yelled out and then fell to the ground.

"Oh my God. Isaac, baby are you okay?" Nina was down on her knees next to her man. He wasn't moving. She bent her head to his chest and then quickly hollered, "Somebody, call 911!"

3

Oh God, no! not again! Not this again! Sweat drizzled from Jude's coal black hair. It dripped from his nose like snot. Could he live through another day of god-awful torment? Evil invaded his space and demanded his attention.

The demon's nostrils flared as he taunted Jude. "You look just like that daddy of yours, so don't think you about to get any sympathy from me." The demon bent down, grabbed a fist full of Jude's collar and threw him against the wall.

"Why is this happening? What do you want?" Jude wanted to fight back. He'd never just took a butt whupping without giving just as good as he got. But he'd tried to fight back down here and it only got worse for him. He needed this to end. When he'd told his dad what he'd been going through, Isaac had told him to always remember to pray whenever he was attacked. But it wasn't stopping nothing. These monsters kept attacking him while he slept. Jude didn't know if he was losing his mind or if this stuff was real and true.

The demon grabbed him by the collar again and swung him into a pile of rotting bones. "I'm going to make you pay for everything your father did to us." The demon cracked his knuckles as he advanced.

"Daddy!" Jude screamed. He needed his dad to come down here and take care of business.

"Your daddy can't help you now. He can't help anyone ever again. Isaac Walker is finally done."

"What are you talking about?" Jude tried to back away from the monster that was sure to tear him from limb to limb, but the pile of bones blocked his exit. He picked up one of the bones, it felt slimy to touch, but he couldn't worry about that right now. There was a big demon baring down on him and he had to fight.

"I'm talking about tearing you to shreds." The demon reached for Jude.

"Leave him alone."

Jude heard the powerful voice. He to terrified to take his eyes off the demon, but at the sound of the man's voice, the demon grew smaller and smaller until he disappeared. Jude lifted his eyes toward a man in the most brilliant white garment he'd ever seen. "Who are you?"

"I am Truth. Follow me."

Truth? Truth who? Jude wanted to know, but the man who had stopped a demon from giving him a royal beat down was leaving, so Jude didn't have time for questions. He got himself off the ground, threw the slimy bones he'd been gripping back into the pile and ran to catch up. "Where are we going?"

"To the fun room," Truth told him.

Yeah right, Jude thought. There was nothing fun about this place. He soon discovered just how right he was.

Truth told him that the Fun Room had been created for those who once enjoyed the pleasures of sin and all its trappings. But as they walked into the room, Jude put a hand over his nose because the so-called 'fun room' smelled of death.

In this room, demons watched as tortured souls tried to recreate the fun they partook in on earth. Crap games were going on. Con artists recited their street hustle over and over again. Former CEOs and executives discussed business ventures.

They were permitted to do anything they wanted in the Fun Room, anything but leave. And that was the rub, because there were also demons in the Fun Room. These demons taunted and tortured their souls. Every hour on the hour a bell would ring. The inhabitants of the Fun Room would tremble with fear and cry out for someone to save them. Jude wondered what was so bad about a bell ringing. He didn't have long to wonder, because the demons grabbed a few unfortunate souls and brought them to the center of the room.

Jude recognized Stephen immediately. Six demons marched around him like he was fresh meat. They hissed and cackled – spit and laughed. Stephen's face was stricken with terror. The demons started poking Stephen with the long spears they carried. They pulled at his flesh. Stephen let out a God-awful scream of agony that tore at Isaac's heart.

Jude turned to Truth. "Help me!"

"I can't, he made his choice. When he was on earth, he chose not to follow God. He even turned you and your other business partner away from your Godly mission."

Yes, okay, that might be true. But even if Stephen had convinced he and Micah to change their app from being a search engine for the Bible to other basic texts books that college kids snapped up and made them rich, he still didn't deserve what was happening to him now. No one did.

"They're going to pull him apart," Jude said as if he was telling Truth something that he couldn't plainly see.

"They often do."

"What do you mean?"

Truth pointed to a pile of discarded limbs. "The demons enjoy mutilating these people. They will pick them apart until there is nothing left."

Jude's eyes widened. "Those bones I touched in the other room were human bones?"

Truth nodded.

The bell rang again Jude watched as Stephen crawled away from the demons. His right arm looked like it had been pulled out of socket. Stephen went back to the group he'd been standing with, they helped him lock his arm back in place as if this was something they did often and it was no big deal.

"Why did you bring me to this room? What can I do to help Stephen? I can't even help myself when those demons come at me."

"Nobody can help him. But time is running out for you. Decide what you're going to do."

"Do? About what?"

Instead of answering, Truth walked away.

Jude tried to catch up. "Don't leave me here. I don't know what you want me to do. Please turn around and talk to me." Jude reached out to touch Truth, but he disappeared. A loud guttural scream escaped Jude as he realized that he just might be stuck in this god-awful place. He called out to Jesus and when that didn't work, he called out to his daddy. Yes, his daddy had the answer. His daddy would be able to help him. He had always helped him.

There came a ringing in his ear, Jude jumped like he was jumping out of his skin. He didn't want to be in the Fun Room when the bell rang. His eyes popped open. Jude's head swiveled from one side to the other. He rubbed his eyes as he realized he was back home on his sofa. But the ringing hadn't stopped. Finally, he caught on to the fact that the phone was ringing. He sat up, looked around, grabbed his cell phone and hit the talk button. "Speak," he barked into the phone.

"Didn't I tell you about answering the phone like that?" Nina yelled into the phone.

His mother never yelled at him. He glanced at the phone as he rubbed his eyes. "Mom, what? I'm sorry, I was sleep."

"I didn't mean to yell. I'm just so upset right now, I'm not myself."

"What's wrong?"

"It's your dad, Jude. I hate to tell you this over the phone but he's had a heart attack."

"No!" He needed his dad. "Please tell me he is not dead?"

"Honey, I'm going to be honest with you. It's touch and go right now. You need to get here as soon as you can."

4

Isaac Walker grew up the hard way. On the streets of Chicago it was kill or be killed and he brought that same knowledge with him to Dayton, Ohio. Back then the only thing Isaac concerned himself with was making money and getting the respect he deserved from those he did business with.

Isaac liked to think of himself as a man of the people back then. He often said that he got along with most living creatures. The only trouble was, to make that statement true, most of Isaac's enemies ended up dead.

The lifestyle he led wasn't a pleasant one. But he'd never wanted anything different, until he met Nina. She was seven years younger than him and had been a college student when they first met. They were as different as two people could be, but that didn't stop him from wanting her.

Little did Isaac know, God had placed Nina in his life and as the years passed, this woman, this gift from God, made him a better man than he ever deserved to be. Nina and Isaac were well into their twilight years, with him being eight-five and she being seventy-eight. Life had been kind to them, but there were times when it seemed so very cruel as well. Like now, while Isaac lay in a hospital bed watching the woman he loved cry as if she were already at his funeral. He couldn't let her feel this kind of pain. Not when they knew what was to come. The

"Woman, what's gotten into you? You're sitting there crying as if we have no hope."

"I... I'm sorry, Isaac." Nina wiped her face with some tissue. "I know that our hope is in the Lord. I just can't stand to see you like this."

"Can't be any worse than the other times I've been laid up in the hospital. But at least this time I don't have a bullet in me."

"Thank God for that. But this issue with your heart isn't any better."

"I've lived a good and long life thanks to you and my Heavenly Father. I'm not complaining, Bae. I'm like any other man. I'd love to keep on living and keep on loving you. But what I'm most worried about now is the work of the ministry. It must continue with or without me."

"And you want to know why I'm crying, but you keep talking like this. Has The Lord told you that He's taking you home and you just haven't told me?"

Isaac shook his head. "No Bae, nothing like that. But I feel tired this time. And I've never felt so tired in all my life."

"Well, you are an old man," Nina laughed despite her tears.

"And I'm finally starting to realize that. Good Lord, I think I'm even ready for you to put those rocking chairs on the front porch like you've been wanting to do."

"Stop talking like this, Isaac. You are scaring me, because you haven't been able to sit still a day in your life."

He nodded, then acknowledged, "Maybe it's time, sit back and rest a little. But don't worry, unless the Lord says different I don't think I'm done living… I still have a lot of atoning to do."

"You've already atoned for everything you did before Christ. God isn't holding you hostage of your past sins, Isaac."

"I hold myself hostage, Nina. I did a lot of wrong… killed a lot of people. They used to haunt me in my sleep. I hated to see how many people I had actually handed over to the devil, because they died before they could make things right with God."

"Rest your mind, Isaac. No sense in troubling yourself about something we can't do anything about."

Isaac closed his eyes, but there would be no rest, the ghosts of his past were visiting him tonight...

Back in the day...

Isaac came of age during the heroine epidemic, and then made his bones during the crack epidemic. Crack was so affordable, that small time hustlers could buy the product, flip it, and flip it until they became kingpins and mafia dogs like the hustlers they had once worked for. That was how the killing started. Everyone wanted a piece of the pie, and all they had to do was gun down the crack king currently on top. But Isaac Walker didn't play that. He had built his organization by sweat, hard work and a bullet if need be. As far as Isaac could see, he wasn't going down, because winners went up.

A lot of hustlers had a problem with how fast he came up in the game. Isaac and Keith had their coat tails pulled and got called out time and time again for taking more than they deserved. But they didn't want nothing that didn't belong to them. So, they agreed to sit down with some of the old heads and listen to their grievances.

Isaac thought that he could shut the old heads up if he could just explain where He and Keith's territory was. At their meeting, however, things did not go so well. No one smiled as Isaac and Keith glanced around the table. Spoony was at the head, Brown was on his right. To Spoony's left was Stevie Johnson. Two other cats were at the table. On Brown's left was another old school hustler named Shinny Watson and next to Stevie was Pete Jones, a guy who came up alongside Isaac. He just wasn't closing as many deals as Isaac of late, but whose fault was that?

"Isaac, your take has doubled in the last year, and some of the brothers here thinking that you're trying to take over?" Spoony told him.

"Have I ever taken anything from you, Spoony?" Isaac asked. Spoony didn't answer so Isaac asked another question. "And don't I still bring all my business to you? So why haven't you already told these cats to lay off?"

Brown said, "Look here sonny-"

Isaac turned his cold black eyes on Brown. "You ain't my daddy, and I'm not your son. I'm a man, and if I speak to you respectfully, I expect the same in return. Understand?"

Brown stood up and exploded. "Boy, I will slit your throat. How's that for respect?"

Spoony touched Brown's arm. "Brown, man, we came here to discuss this like reasonable men. Sit down, please."

Brown flopped back into his seat as he told Spoony, "You just better tell your boy to check his self, before I do it for him."

Stevie put his elbows on the table and tried his hand at intimidation. "Isaac, people are concerned."

Brown added, "And we are all a little worried about your family's safety. People are getting uptight, thinking that you and Keith are earning money that should have been theirs. Anything could happen."

Isaac wanted to laugh in Brown's face. The only family he had left was his usually-wrong daddy and he would gladly give up the address to Usually-wrong's house if they wanted to do him a favor and kill that maggot. Thank God and good reddens was how Isaac saw it.

But Keith was another matter. He stood up and told them, "If you think I'm going to sit here and listen to you threaten my family, you've got another thought coming. Bring it on," Keith said as he strutted to the door and waited on Isaac to join him.

Isaac slowly rose out of his chair, understanding he had now entered a game of winner take all – loser eat six feet of dirt. He nodded at Spoony and said, "I'll see you around."

Spoony nodded back with a look on his face that said, "I sure hope so."

Over the next three months, Isaac and Keith's cars were bombed. Their homes were riddled with bullets, so they started moving from hotel to hotel. Their runners were gunned down in the street. Isaac and Keith went to war and hit them harder than they were hit. By the end of that three month period, Stevie, Shinny and Pete were no longer of this world. The only two that were at that round table meeting left alive besides Isaac and Keith were Spoony and Brown. Spoony had arranged a meeting with Isaac and Brown and had them both agree to end the war. Isaac willingly agreed to stay on his side of town and leave Brown to his side. And with that, it was over. But, just when Isaac and Keith thought they could breathe easy again, two things happened.

Leonard came home when Isaac was at Clara's bringing some money to help with the bills. He'd stolen her bill money that month and the month before *and they were getting ready to be evicted. Leonard walked over to Isaac as he sat at the kitchen table playing with his godson and said, "I miss you, man. How you just gon' drop me like this when we supposed to be boys."*

Isaac handed the baby back to Clara and told Leonard, "There's no place in my organization for crack-heads."

Leonard started jumping around the kitchen like a man without hope, flailing his long arms and kicking in the air. He turned back to Isaac and pulled at his worn and tattered clothes and asked, "Do you think I want to be like this?"

"We warned you more times than I can count about sampling the product. Is it my fault that you wouldn't listen?"

Leonard walked over to Isaac and got on his knees. "Help me, man. Don't you see me? Look at me, Isaac. I need help!"

Isaac was saddened by the man that knelt before him. Leonard's cheeks were sunken and he had the ashen look that crack-heads get. His boy had sunken low and Isaac sat on the sidelines while it happened. "I'll tell you what," Isaac began. "If you agree to go to rehab, then I'll have your back all the way."

Leonard stood up and stepped away from Isaac. "Ah man, them rehabs don't work. Why you want to make me waist time like that when I could be back on the block helping you?"

"If you're serious about getting clean, it'll work. Take it or leave it."

Leonard tried to reason with Isaac but Isaac, grabbed his keys and walked out of the house with one last parting remark to Leonard. "Have Clara call me when you check into rehab. I'll send you some roses."

Isaac received a call from Joey, one of his runners. Joey told him that Keith needed to get over to his mother's apartment a-sap. Isaac got Keith on the phone and told him, "Man, you need to get over to your mom's place. Something has happened."

"I told you I don't want to be bothered by her drama anymore?" Keith said.

"You need to get over there, Keith. One of my runners just called and told me that the ambulance and police are at her place."

When they hung up, Isaac sped towards Ms. Doretha's apartment on the lower South Side. He pulled up at the same time Keith did. He watched as Keith jumped out of his car and ran up to one of the police officers. Then Keith turned and watched the paramedics bringing the bed out of the apartment with a body bag on top of it. He ran over to them. The police officer followed, trying to hold him back.

"Get off me, man. That's my Mama," Keith yelled as he trotted forward.

The paramedics set the ambulatory bed down and stood in front of it, waving Keith away. "You don't want to see her now, sir," One of them told him.

Isaac ran over to Keith and tried to pull him away also. But Keith jerked away. "I have a right to know if that is my mother." Keith pointed at the body bag.

"She's been cut up, man. Don't do this to yourself," the other police officer said.

Keith grabbed the bag and quickly unzipped it before he could be stopped by anyone. A thin arm fell out, but Keith wasn't looking at the arm. He was looking into the slashed and bloody face of Doretha Williams. He put his arms around her and became covered in blood because her chest was cut-up as well. Keith didn't notice how bloody he was becoming. He just wanted to hold his mother one last time. "I'm sorry. You hear me?" he asked her. "I'm sorry."

Isaac pulled Keith off of his mother so the paramedics could close the bag back up. Keith tried to fall back on the body, but Isaac grabbed him. Tears were streaming down Keith's face as Isaac hugged him. Isaac's own mother had been carried out by the paramedics covered in blood. So as they hugged, Isaac and Keith became forever bonded in blood.

"Come on, man. Let me take you home," Isaac said.

"No. I can't leave her like this, Isaac. She needs me, man."

"You've got to get out of here. Let these people do their job." Isaac tried to pull Keith away again, and this time Keith allowed him. He took Keith over to his car and opened the passenger side door for him. "Get in, Keith. I'll have Valerie come pick up your car."

Keith sat in the car numbly as Isaac drove. He then clenched his fist and smashed it against the dashboard. "Brown did this. I know it in my gut."

Isaac didn't say anything, but he had been thinking over the probability of Brown having something to do with Keith's mother's death. Ms. Doretha had been prostituting to get her drugs. Anyone could have done this as far as Isaac was concerned.

"We should have killed him right along with the rest of them."

"Well, I'll tell you what," Isaac said. "Let's check into it, and if Brown had something to do with this, then his family will finally get to cash in his insurance policy.

~~~~

As it turned out, the killer just about begged the police to come and get him. He'd left his fingerprints all over Doretha's apartment and body and bragged to numerous friends about the murder. Michael Hopkins was arrested in a coffee shop that was owned by Brown. And it was no wonder that the murderer was arrested at Brown's coffee shop, since he was one of Brown's top soldiers.

Keith and Isaac were watching the news while Valerie fixed steaks for them. The arrest was televised, so after watching Michael Hopkins get carted out of Brown's coffee shop, Isaac and Keith looked at each other and nodded. That night they went out in search of Brown and whoever might try to get in their way. They found him at Fat Al's juke joint. It was ten at night so there was only four people in the joint; Fat Al, Brown and two of Brown's henchmen. Brown was sitting at a back table sucking on a barbecue rib bone. His men were at the bar. Isaac and Keith sat at Brown's table and trained their guns on him from underneath the table.

46

"Isaac told Brown, "You shouldn't have done it.""

Brown put his barbecue down and asked, "What are you talking about?"

"We hadn't tried to move in on your operation. We hadn't bothered anything of yours, but the way you had Keith's mother cut up." Isaac shook his head and then finished with, "We can't let that go."

Brown turned to Keith. "I didn't do anything to your mother. Don't act crazy and get yourself killed in here."

"Brave talk for a dead man," Isaac said.

Brown laughed in Isaac's face. "Man, get out of here before you get hurt."

"We never forgot how you warned us about our family, Brown," Keith said.

"And now we've got a warning for you," Isaac said, and then pulled the trigger and shot Brown in the gut.

Brown began lifting out of his chair. "You can't shoot me," he said.

But Isaac must not have understood him because he lifted his gun and shot him again; this time in the head. As Brown fell face forward on top of his barbecue, Keith shot two of Brown's henchmen as they tried to pull out their guns.

"What's up, Fat Al," Isaac asked as he pointed his gun at him.

Fat Al raised his hands. "I'm not taking sides, Ike-man. I've got a family and I just want to get out of here and see them again."

"You remember your family when the police ask you about this. Okay?" Isaac said as he and Keith backed out the door.

5

Jude hadn't been able to get a flight out of Los Angeles until the next morning. He'd left his house at five a.m. for a seven a.m. flight. Alexa still hadn't come home by the time he left and he didn't bother to leave her a note because as far as he was concerned, it was over. No need to leave a note for that.

What had caused Alexa to think that she could stay out on him all night and still have a home to come back to, Jude didn't know. But she would soon discover that she played herself. He would have her stuffed moved back to her apartment while he was in Ohio, but for right now his only thoughts were of his father.

The formidable Isaac Walker had fallen. He'd been struck down by the ticking time bomb inside of him. Jude had wanted to talk to his father for weeks. But he'd avoided calls or made excuses for why he couldn't talk long, all because of the doubts that had been plaguing him since Stephen's untimely death.

If his father died before he could get to him and thank him for being the man he was... the man who taught him how to stand on his own two feet and become a man in this world that his family could be proud of. But lately, Jude hadn't been proud of himself. Micah had been right, he had sold out his values as he'd tried to forget everything that God had put in his heart... things he was called to do.

As he landed in Ohio, Jude prayed that his father was still alive. He needed the old man to give him a good kick in the rear one more time. He got off the plane and waited for his luggage. His cell phone rang and Jude saw that it was Alexa. He really didn't want to talk to her, but he wanted her packed and out of his house before he got back home, so he answered the phone.

"Jude, hon, I know you're at work, but I just wanted to let you know that I'm okay. My car got a flat tire last night so I just stayed over at Darlene's house. I knew you wouldn't want me out in the middle of the night trying to get a tire fixed."

He didn't even care enough to ask why she didn't call him or triple A. "I'm not at work. I'm in Ohio. My father had a heart attack last night."

"Oh Jude, I'm so sorry. If you would have waited for me to get home, I would have flown out there with you."

"Don't worry about it."

"I just don't want you coming back here even more depressed than you already are. I couldn't take it if you moped around here one more day."

"When I said don't worry about it. I meant that you don't have to worry about any of it, because I want you out of my house before I get back to town."

"What?"

"You heard me."

"You don't mean that."

"Oh but I do. Pack you stuff and take it back to your apartment. You can leave my key on the table in the foyer."

"So, you're that mad about me not coming home last night? Can you blame me for not wanting to be here with the way you've been acting lately?"

"I don't blame you, Alexa. I'm just done. It is over between us."

"I wasn't out fooling around last night if that's what you think."

"Alexa, listen to me and listen good. I don't care who you were with last night. Go be with them again tonight. But do it after you pack your stuff and get out of my house." He hung up and kept it moving.

When Jude arrived at the hospital, his brother Donavan and sister Iona were seated in the waiting area of the intensive care unit. He hugged both of them.

Iona kissed him on the cheek. "I sure have missed seeing your big head around here."

With his dad in the hospital and the fact that he hadn't been keeping in touch lately, Jude felt guilty about his actions. Lowering his head, he admitted, "I should call more, I know."

"Call, and visit," Donavan chided.

His brother and sister could get on his case all they wanted, but before their conversation went any further, Jude had to know... "How's dad?"

Smiling, Iona said, "Last night was touch and go. But he's responding to the medicine the doctor gave him."

"Will they let me in to see him?"

"Momma's in there with him right now. As soon as she comes back out here, you should be able to go in." Donavan told him, then added, "Dad will be real glad to see you. This might be the boost he needs right now."

"I thought you said he's doing better? I didn't come all the way back here just to watch my father die."

"Calm down, Ikee." Iona put a hand over her mouth then released it. "I keep forgetting that you're a grown man with your own identity now."

"You can call me Ikee, Sis. I don't mind. It's not as if I don't like my name. I just needed to differentiate myself from the great Isaac Walker as I was building my own identity in the business world."

"We understand that, Donavan said as he palmed Jude's head as if it were a basketball.

"Don't start that stuff," Jude told him as he backed away from his brother.

"Oh, you too grown for that too, huh." Donavan shook his head. "I want my little brother who went off to college vowing to stay the same."

"Don't listen to him," Iona said as she stood in between her brothers. "You've done good. My kids are even using your Find It app to do some of their homework."

Jude gave a weak smile at Iona's praise, because no matter how much good that app has done with kids in school, he knew in his heart that it wasn't doing what it was originally designed to do.

The doors to the ICU opened, Nina walked into the waiting area, but as she looked up to see her youngest son, her eyes misted and she stopped in her tracks. "Son."

"I'm here, Mama. I'm here." Jude rushed to Nina's side.

Nina wrapped her arms around her son and began rapidly speaking in a language that Jude could not interpret. She was speaking in tongues. Her body shook as if she had caught the Holy Ghost and was about to dance down the aisle of the waiting room. "My son, my son," she finally said once she began speaking in her native tongue again. "How we have missed you."

"I'm sorry I didn't come home sooner Mama. If I would have known that daddy was sick, I would have. I promise I would have."

"It's not too late Judah. Your father is still alive, so the two of you can make peace and then you can deal with whatever it is that is keeping you away from us."

Jude wished with everything that was in him that what his mother said was true. But he didn't know how to tell her that it wasn't his earthly father he needed to make peace with. And until he could finally come to terms with how he must has disappointed his Heavenly Father, Jude didn't see how there could be much peace.

6

"Why did you scare me like that, Old Man? You and mom are supposed to stay alive long enough to babysit for me. It's only fair… I mean, y'all been watching Donavan's and Iona's big head kids all this time," Jude joked with Isaac.

"You got a kid on the way that I don't know about?" Isaac side-eyed him.

"I certainly do not, so that means you'll have to live a long time, at least until I can find the woman I'm going to marry, settle down and have some kids with her."

"What about that woman you been shacking up with. You do know that kids come from what you're doing, right?"

"Alexa and I broke up, Dad. I'm not shacking with anybody. And don't try to change the subject, because I want you around to babysit each child that I have. You owe it to me. And I don't want to feel like

I'm getting short changed just because you were ready for a rocking chair by the time I was born."

The heart attack had weakened Isaac, but he had enough strength to laugh at his son's foolishness. "Watch your mouth boy. Rocking chairs have never been my style."

"Oh yeah, I heard that you just told mom to put a couple on the front porch. Your not going soft on me, are you?"

"Not going soft, son. Just got old all of a sudden."

Jude plopped down in the chair next to his father's hospital bed. Seeing his father laid low like this, with IVs, a heart monitor and an oxygen tank was devastating to Jude because his father had always been larger than life to him.

"Now look whose going soft." Isaac pointed at Jude.

A tear drifted down his face as he said, "Do you expect me to be happy while you're in here sounding like it's the end?"

Patting his son's shoulder, Isaac told him, "I want to be here to see all of my grandchildren come into this world too, son. But if God wants to take me home, then that's His business. I'm going to be all right either way. What you really need to be concerned with is what's next for you? Because I'm not always going to be around to knock some sense into your head. So, you need to jump on the get right train whether I'm here or not... understand me?"

"But what if I still need you to knock me upside the head every once in a while?"

Isaac smirked at that. "I think I did my job well enough that you'll remember." And indeed he had. Back when Jude allowed his family to call him Ikee, he'd become a wanna-be thug and Isaac had to show him that he really didn't want the lifestyle he thought he wanted.

Isaac was far from a street thug by the time Jude came along. But by the time Jude became a teenager and tried to test the waters, he soon discovered that the street thugs still didn't want no trouble from his father and neither did he...

Isaac stepped into Bobby-Ray's trap house like he had paid the mortgage on the joint. Hustlers and geekers were sprawled out all around the room. He took his time, looking each person in the face and saying a silent prayer for each person as he passed them. The devil couldn't hold the captives bound forever... not when the saints were praying.

"You looking for somebody?"

Isaac swung around and came face to face with Bobby-Ray. He knew it was him, because except for the excess weight, Bobby-Ray looked just like his father. A man Isaac had ignorantly murdered and then had to watch Ray-Ray being tortured in Hell. Of course Isaac felt bad about what he'd done to Bobby-Ray's daddy, but not bad enough to let him have his son. "You're the man I'm looking for. You and my son, that is," Isaac told him.

"What do I have to do with your son?"

"You need to explain that to me. Because the way I got it, you've been telling my son stories that his ears were never meant to hear."

With a sinister grin on his face, Bobby-Ray said, "I didn't know that you being a murdering, thieving parasite was such a secret."

"Where's my son?" Isaac asked, ignoring the obvious taunt.

Bobby-Ray stood his ground. Kept smirking in Isaac's face.

Isaac took a step closer. "Careful, young man. You only know what you heard about me, but I'm way more lethal than that. Don't make me prove it to you."

Bobby-Ray swallowed the lump in his throat as he stepped aside and then pointed to a room in the back.

Isaac didn't have anyone to watch his back like he did in the old days when he and Keith would roll up on hustlers and take care of business. But Isaac wasn't worried because God had his back these days. He headed into the next room and immediately spotted his son handing a rock to a woman and then taking the money from her and putting it in his pocket. What Isaac saw turned his stomach. He had worked long and hard, just about moved heaven and earth to keep his son away from this kind of life.

When Isaac had been drafted into this life, it had been because he couldn't think of any other way to make a quick buck. His mother and brother sat at home starving because his daddy was out drinking up all the money. So, Isaac had to make things happen. But even with all the advantages his son had, Ikee still wanted to be the dope man. The thought sent Isaac into a rage as he put holy hands on Ikee and knocked him against the filthy wall, which probably hadn't been washed in years.

Isaac's arm was against Ikee's neck. He applied pressure, wanting to choke him out. Ikee desperately tried to claw the arm away, but Isaac would not be moved and Ikee was about to black out. "I'm only going to tell you this once," Isaac said as he spoke in Ikee's left ear. "I'm walking out of this god-awful place and driving home. When I get there my wife's car had better be back in the garage."

"How did Ikee beat you home?" Nina asked Isaac as he walked through the door.

"He was motivated," was all Isaac told her as he strode up the stairs. He grabbed a suitcase out of his and Nina's walk-in closet. He then stalked over to Ikee's door and swung it open without knocking.

"Hey man, this is my room," Ikee said as he hopped off his bed.

"You don't have a room in my house anymore." Isaac threw the suitcase at him. "Pack your stuff."

"Why I got to pack? Where am I supposed to go?"

Nina rushed to the room. "Isaac, what's going on? You can't just throw him out. He's not even eighteen yet." And besides, this was her baby.

"He's a drug dealer, Nina. He can't stay here because his very existence put you and the rest of our family at risk." Isaac turned a cold stare on Ikee. "But you don't care nothing about that, do you?"

"You trippin'. It's not like I killed anybody. I'm just trying to flip a few dollars so I can buy my Mustang."

"Ikee!" Nina's hand went to her mouth as she shook her head. "Why would you need to do something like that? Your father and I provide everything you need."

"You said that I had to get a car with the money I have or find a way to earn enough to get the car that I want."

"We certainly never asked you to go sell drugs," Nina declared, still very clearly devastated by the news she'd just received.

"How did you think I was going to get my Mustang then? Nobody here was going to help me. So, I had to get my hustle on. I don't really see the big deal. Dad sold drugs for years. That's probably why we have this four-thousand-square-foot home and the cars."

"First of all, you don't have a four-thousand-square-foot home; me and your mom own this home and the cars. Drug money didn't buy any of it. Everything we have is because of the Lord's mercy and grace. And I'm not about to allow a drug dealer to sully any of it." Isaac pointed at the suitcase. "Make sure you only take shoes and clothes. That Xbox and your iPad stay here."

Ikee picked up his cell phone and quickly called his sister. When she answered he started mouthing off,

"Your daddy is throwing me out; can I crash over there until I can get a place of my own?"

Isaac snatched the phone from Ikee. He put it to his ear as he told Iona, "The only place your brother is going to end up in is a jail cell or a pine box. He's a drug dealer, Iona. And he can't stay at your house. I won't allow him to put my grandchildren at risk."

"But Daddy, he's just a kid. Where's he going to go if he can't stay with family?"

"That's for this little ninja to figure out. He wants to be a king pin, well maybe a dose of living on the streets will give him a good start so he can learn how to be hard and tough enough for his chosen career." He hung up with Iona and then put Ikee's iPhone in his pocket.

Jude had been sixteen when he introduced him to the I-don't-play Isaac Walker. Now as Isaac lay on his sick bed, not able to do much of anything, he was thankful that he had knocked some sense into Jude's head at a young age. Because after living on his own and experiencing all that the street life had to offer, Jude had turned his life around within a week. The battle had been hard fought, but Isaac snatched his son from the streets.

Jude might not be where God wanted him right now, but the boy would come around, Isaac was sure of it. Because he, better than anyone that the prayers of the righteous avails much, and Isaac kept praying that God would lead Jude home.

7

The nurse came in and told Jude that Isaac needed rest. Jude needed a little time to calm down anyway, so he stepped out of his father's room and went back to the waiting room. Nina walked over to her son and gave him a hug.

"Your eyes are red, have you been crying?" she asked as they walked back toward the family.

"I just don't like the way he's talking... like he doesn't have any fight left in him."

"Don't fool yourself, Jude. Your daddy will fight with his last breath to stay here with us. He just wants us to know that either way things turn out, he'll be okay."

Jude couldn't help himself, he looked his mother in the eye and asked, "Are you okay with this, no matter which way it turns out."

Nina thought about that for a moment and then answered, "I've been loving your father for a long time. I don't think I'll ever be ready to say goodbye to that man. But I'll shed my tears now, because when that day comes I'm going to be too busy rejoicing for my husband's entry into heaven."

Jude wrestled with this thought of being okay with death when there was so much living left to do. Sure, his father was eighty-five and had lived a long life, but Jude wanted him to keep on living and save all the 'well-dones' for another time.

He was about to tell his mother that, but they were now back in the area where Iona and Donavan had been seated before he went into the ICU to visit with his father. But before he could open his mouth, his eyes scanned the area and noted that Johnny, Iona's husband and Diana, Donavan's wife were now in the waiting room. But that wasn't what stopped him in his tracks. Marissa Allen, the girl who stole his heart and threw it back at him was also in the waiting area.

As Jude sat down next to Nina, Keith and Cynda, long-time friends of the family, oh and yeah, Cynda was Iona's birth mother. So, at one time, Cynda and his dad had gotten together. Since Donavan was older than Iona, Jude had put two and two together, without ever asking his parents about it. Because he figured that was probably a subject his mom didn't want to dwell on, especially since she and Cynda were such good friends now. But at one time, his dad had been a serious mac.

Nina hopped up and hugged Cynda and Keith. "You two were out here pretty late last night. I thought you'd be resting today."

"Not a chance, I had to come and let the old geezer see how good I'm getting around and get him jealous enough to get out of his sick bed," Keith told Nina.

But Keith wasn't as steady as he used to be. His body shook as he spoke and he now walked with a cane. Jude still remembered when Keith and his father ran revivals from city to city. During summer breaks from college, Jude traveled with his father and Keith, passing out flyers and watching as they preached the gospel to a hurting nation. But once he graduated and started his own business, Jude didn't have time for revivals.

He always thought that he'd hang out with his father on one of those revivals again someday. But three years ago they held the last revival and hadn't scheduled another since. "Hey Uncle Keith and Aunt Cynda." Jude gave them hugs.

"Look at you," Cynda said. "It's been so long since I saw you, I almost forgot what you look like."

"The boy looks just like his daddy. I'd recognize him in a crowd with his back turned." Keith nudged Jude. "I'm sure it did your father's heart good to see you."

Why did he say it like that? Jude already felt bad for not visiting his family much in the last few years. But somehow, Keith's words caused tears to form in Jude's eyes. "I'm going to step outside for a minute. Please let me know if the doctor comes out to talk to us," he told the group as he rushed out.

Once he was outside Jude roared like a wounded animal as he balled his fist and hit the brick building as if he was Sampson and could bring a building down with the might of his hands. With tears in his eyes, Jude looked to heaven. He wanted to pray and ask God to forgive him for turning his back on his faith and his family, but he felt so ashamed of the way he'd been living his life these past few years, that Jude didn't know if he could go to God in prayer anymore.

His mom taught him about loving God, but his dad taught him how to be a man and how to serve God. Jude had gone on about his way, worrying more about becoming a successful businessman than being a part of his family. Now his father had suddenly gotten old and Jude didn't know how much time he had to make up for ignoring the man who raised him.

He leaned against the wall and immediately felt a hand on his shoulder. Then he heard, "Are you okay, Jude?"

Her voice was like a melody that one could play over and over and never get tired of hearing it. But that same voice had put cracks in Jude's heart. So, Jude didn't turn around. Too many emotions were going through him, and he didn't trust himself not to do something stupid.

Marissa wasn't to be put off. "I know you're hurting Jude. I just want to help, if I can."

He shoved his hands in his pockets as he turned to face her. "How can you help me?"

She shrugged. "I probably can't do much. But I do have a shoulder you can lean on. If that's what you need right now."

Jude remembered coming to Marissa a few years back and proudly telling her about the fortune he'd made and explaining that he would now be able to take care of her. All he had asked was that they live together for at least six month before getting married. He only wanted to make sure that they were truly compatible for one another. But Marissa didn't understand that.

After college, Marissa had come back home and now headed up an outreach program for at-risk youth at the church. Marissa felt that she would be turning her back on her faith if she shacked up with him before marriage. Then she even questioned his faith. Finally, she informed him that since they were obviously going in different directions that she could no longer sit at home waiting on him to come to his senses.

Marissa had then started dating Lou Marshall, one of the elders at his father's church. As far as Jude was concerned Lou was too young to be an elder. Lou was only four years older than he. Jude had thought of Lou as a friend but the man had stolen his woman so that friendship was over. "How's Lou?"

"I'm sure he's fine. But I didn't come out here to talk about Lou. I know how close you and your father are, and I know it's hard for you to see him like this."

Jude shook his head. "We used to be close. But I've been so busy building my business these last few years that I haven't been around much."

"We've missed you at church."

The words didn't sound condemning coming from Marissa. More like she really missed seeing him at church. He was disarmed by her comment and could only admit the truth. "I wish I had come back home more. Maybe I should have been attending church. But I guess I got caught up."

"I'm sure your family is glad that you're home now."

"Yeah, but look what it took to get me on that plane." Jude turned his back to Marissa, too disgusted with himself to look her in the eye. "I just wish I had been around more."

"You had to make your own way in the world... no shame in that."

Jude closed his eyes trying to block out the pain his heart was enduring because Marissa was so close to him. He had wanted to make a life with this woman, but she preferred another. A man who had given his life to serve God, while Jude had been serving himself. Just thinking of Marissa with Elder Lou made Jude feel small and useless. He couldn't bear to be so close to her and not be able to touch her or claim her for his own.

Marissa wouldn't back up, she stood in front of him, and put a hand on his chest. "Stop torturing yourself, Jude. Your father is going to pull through. God is not done with Pastor Walker yet."

"I believe that," he told her without admitting what he'd been thinking about. "My dad is not allowed to die. He's been slacking on his ministry for three years now. It's time for him to get back out there and rile up people to accept the Lord." Jude puffed out his chest trying to look and stand like his father as he delivered the word of God. "Count up the cost, young man. Either you're going to live for God or die with the devil you're currently serving."

Marissa laughed as she playfully shoved Jude's shoulder. "I remember him saying that. It was at the first revival I ever attended. His words made me realize that I not only wanted, but needed to serve the Lord. So, don't make fun of my pastor and his passion for saving souls."

"I'm the one who knocked on your door that day, so don't give him all the credit." He was glad that he'd done that for her because she seemed happier now than she had been back then. God looked good on her.

"Thank you for helping to rescue me, Jude. I've never forgotten what you did for me at a time I needed it most."

"Thanks for coming out here with me. I'm starting to feel better about things. But you might want to get back in there. I wouldn't want Lou to come to the hospital and see you out here with me."

Giving him a kind-of-sort-of smile, Marissa said, "You haven't been home in a long time. So, let me be upfront with you. Lou and I aren't seeing each other anymore. He's engaged to someone else."

"Then he's a fool," Jude said without thinking. He didn't know why, but the thought of Lou breaking up with Marissa for some other woman angered him. Lou had never been good enough for his Marissa, and to think the man now had the nerve to decide that he wanted someone else.

Marissa waved his words off. "Lou and Stacey are perfect for each other. Trust me, there are no hard feelings between us. He made the right decision."

Was Marissa now with another man? Is that why she wasn't so concerned about Lou marrying someone else. Jude was just about to quiz her about her love life when Donavan rushed outside and beckoned to them.

"The doctor wants to talk to us about dad. You need to come back inside.

8

"That's good news," Nina said to the doctor as Jude walked back into the waiting area.

"What's good news?" Jude wanted to know.

As Nina turned to him, tears were flowing down her face. She hugged him. "Your dad is responding to the medication."

The doctor added. "I don't want to get your hopes up. He seems to be responding… we won't know for sure for several days. But if he doesn't suffer a setback tonight, we'll move him out of the ICU tomorrow."

Shouts and "Thank You Jesus's" went up. Nina let go of Jude and hugged Donavan and Iona. Jude was so excited that he picked Marissa up, swung her around and then wrapped her in his arms like she belonged to him and hugged her as if he never wanted to let her go.

"It's okay, Jude. I told you that your father was going to be all right."

Marissa speaking into his ear brought him back to the moment. They were in the ICU, the doctor had just told them that his father was doing better... he was holding Marissa in his arms, but she didn't belong there. Jude released her and stepped back. His hands went in his pocket again. "Thank you, for coming out here to be with my family. You're a good friend."

"I will always be your friend, Jude. I hope you know that."

Oh, he knew it... knew it better than he knew his name. Marissa had forever relegated him to the friend zone, and since he had been living with another woman until yesterday, there was no way that he could complain about that. "Yeah, I know," he told her as he turned back to his family.

"I knew that husband of mine wasn't ready to check out of here just yet," Nina said as they all sat back down.

"I knew Isaac wasn't going anywhere. That one will be fighting death with his last breath," Keith told the group.

"I don't know about that, Uncle Keith," Donavan said. "It was touch and go last night. He didn't look like the same bigger than life man that I have loved and feared most of my life. I really thought I was about to say goodbye to my daddy."

Jude thought the same thing also. But it didn't have anything to do with how his father looked. By the time he had reached the hospital, his father had already been showing signs of improving. But he seemed at peace with whatever was about to happen to him.

Jude was amazed about that. He remembered how his father had preached on countless occasions that to be absent from the body was to be present with the Lord. Isaac would always make it sound as if when people who were saved by God's grace passed from this life, they weren't truly dying, because they would live again.

Jude often wondered if his father believed the words that he preached, after seeing him and hearing him talk of going home, as if God had some ready-made home in heaven for him, Jude now knew that Isaac Walker believed every word he'd preached. Jude then admitted to the group, "Dad scared me out of my mind when I visited with him early. It wasn't that he looked as if he might die... but that it didn't seem to matter one way or the other to him. I guess I just don't understand how a man who claims to love his family like Dad does, could be so ready to leave us like that."

Nina moved over a seat so that she was next to Jude. She gently put a hand on his shoulder as she shook her head. "Your daddy isn't anxious to leave us. But know this, if Isaac Walker died today, we would be sad, but he would be rejoicing in heaven, because my husband is a man of God. He has given his life for the cause of Christ. And I just wish I could be there to see My Lord and Savior say, '*Well done, good and faithful servant; you were faithful over a few things, I will make you ruler over many things. Enter into the joy of Your Lord*'."

Jude didn't like the sound of that. "For you to be able to hear that, you'd have to die with dad, and I don't think I could take losing both of you at the same time." What had he been thinking... staying away from his family so long? His mother had been fifty when he was born. But both, his mother and father had always looked so young and vibrant that he never thought much about their age. They weren't looking so young these days though.

"Don't go crying on us baby-boy. Mama-Nina and Daddy ain't going nowhere anytime soon," Iona told him in her needling way.

"I'm not no baby-boy. I'm a full grown man and I've been taking care of myself for years now, so you need to put some respect on my name."

Iona got up and mugged him in the head. "Boy, I helped change your diapers so you are always going to be baby-boy to me."

"And I taught you how to tie your shoes. That took forever because you didn't care about tripping on those shoe laces… drove me crazy," Donavan said.

"And don't let me tell everybody how long it took you to stop wetting the bed," Nina chimed in," enjoying the moment with her grown kids.

"What? Do tell, First Lady," Marissa poked fun at Jude. "How long did he stay in diapers?"

Jude jumped out of his seat. "Okay, that's enough." He waved his hands in the air, trying to end the craziness. "I was out of diapers at two and I rarely wet the bed. End of story."

"If you say so." Nina turned her head away from Jude and laughed, which caused everybody else to start laughing as well.

Everybody but Jude. "I see how this is going. I haven't been home in a while, so y'all want to gang up on me. But I know some secrets too. So, who wants me to tell what I know. Next person to tell a Jude joke, gets outed." They became so silent that the shuffling of papers could be heard from three feet away at the nurses station. "Yeah, I didn't think y'all wanted to mess with me."

~~~~

Off into the far, far away distance, angels in heaven were looking down on the Walker family. Brogan and Arnoth stood before the captain of the host. Their wings were folded and their spirits were downcast.

"I don't think I've ever seen warrior angels look as sad as the two of you."

"I'm not ready for my assignment to end." Brogan confessed to Captain Aaron.

Nodding, Captain Aaron acknowledged. "He's been one of the best. But that's the thing about humans, they cannot keep their earthly body forever. It must go back to the dust and the spirit must go where it belongs."

Arnoth put an arm around Brogan's shoulder. "We know that Isaac's spirit will rise up to heaven, so whichever way this turns out, he will live on forever."

"I know… I've just been standing here reminiscing about the exploits of Isaac Walker. He fought a good fight and brought many souls to the Lord. My one saving grace is that one day soon I will finally get a chance to shake his hand. That will be a great day."

"There's no telling when that day will actually be, so I'm sending you and Arnoth back to earth on another assignment," Captain Aaron told them.

"Surely Isaac isn't about to take on another exploit, the man is barely able to lift his head." Brogan shook his head while looking down to earth, longing to be able to do battle for Isaac on the Lord's behalf just one more time.

"Look a little deeper my friend. You and Arnoth will battle the enemy very soon, but it will be for Isaac Judah Walker and Marissa Allen."

Their frowns were replaced by the brightest smile this side of heaven, as Brogan and Arnoth realized that God wasn't done with this family yet. They lifted their swords and shouted with a loud voice, "We will fight for all that is good and all that is right."

~~~~

Isaac still felt weak and could barely lift his head from his pillow the next morning. But they moved him out of ICU, so Isaac figured he had to be doing better than he was feeling. The added bonus was that he was able to have his family in his room. Nina was still monitoring his visits and requesting that the kids not hang out in the room all day long.

Isaac found himself sleeping so much that he didn't know who was in the room on that first day anyway. He'd never been much for lying in the bed, sleeping the day away when there was so much work yet to be done. He'd told friends and family whenever they suggested that he get some more sleep or that he needed to rest, "I'll sleep when I'm dead. But this is the day the Lord has made, and I'm going to make some noise every day He sees fit to wake me up."

The trouble with getting old was that Isaac still didn't feel old. Of course he felt tired and sick right now, but before his heart attack, Isaac had still been on the go. He'd been out there chasing down souls and winning them for the kingdom of God. Admittedly, he had slowed down. His bones now ached and quaked in places he'd never felt pain before. He and Keith were no longer doing their street revivals, because they couldn't figure how to get it to the next level. Which was strange, because Isaac had moved so many obstacles out of his way in order to get the work of God done. But he just couldn't make since of why he couldn't get out of his own way and work the ministry God gave him.

These days it wasn't visits to Hell that kept him up at night anymore. Matter-of-fact, Isaac hadn't been drug into Satan's kingdom in many years. He wasn't complaining, because there had been times when Isaac thought he would lose his mind if he had to witness another human being tortured. But it pained him that his son was now going through so much torment. Jude would need to figure out what the Lord needed from him if the torment was to ever stop.

Isaac didn't know what God was up to. Didn't know whether it was a gift or a curse to be able to see into the spiritual realm the way he and Jude could. But one thing he did know, was that even though he wasn't witnessing torture in Devil Land these days, everywhere Isaac looked, he still saw so much trouble in the world. His work was not finished, but it was as if God was diminishing his hunger to get out there and do something about this hurting world. He was decreasing, Isaac understood that, but who was meant to take his place? Jude certainly didn't want anything to do with the evangelistic ministry. Donavan was busy with the church, Iona had her family and her work as an attorney that she loved.

So, Isaac was not tormented at the fact that he had unfinished business, but didn't know who would be willing to finish it for him. That is what Isaac mostly spent his time praying about these days... that God would send a man, on fire for the Lord that he could groom to take over for him.

Isaac turned his head to the left as he felt a movement in his room. No one was there, at least no one that he could see in the natural. Isaac smiled yet and still, because he could feel the anxiety leaving him. His angel was in the room with him, working things out even as Isaac thought and prayed about them.

Sighing deeply, Isaac said out loud, "I'd like to see you before I die." And as he laid there getting comfortable in his bed for the first time since arriving at the hospital, Isaac thought how wonderful it would be if men could see the angels that God sends to protect them. How glorious would something like that be?

9

Most of the family had left for the night, it was only Jude, Nina and Isaac now in his hospital room. Since he'd had that last experience in Hell, Jude had wanted to talk to his dad about his experiences. But now that Isaac was sick, he didn't know if he should bring it up. The television was on CNN, and just as Jude had convinced himself that this was not a good time to bother his father with what he was going through, something terrible happened.

CNN was showing a video of a man who had his hands up, walking backward away from several police officers. Once the man reached his car, he put his hands on his car and then was shot down just as if he had actually done something that warranted a deadly bullet.

Nina, Isaac and Jude's mouths hung open as they watched and listened. Apparently the man's car had broken down and instead of the police offering assistance, they immediately assumed that 'this guy was a real bad dude', as one of the officers flying in the helicopter above could be heard saying.

Nina stood up and walked toward the television, as if she would see something different if she moved a little closer. "What just happened? Tell me I didn't just see what my lying eyes are telling me?"

"I wish I could. But it's happening right in front of us." Jude's nostril's flared. His fist clenched as red hot rage went through his body.

Isaac couldn't get out of bed, but as he laid there shaking his head, he told them, we need to pray. Something terrible is about to happen. I feel it in my bones."

Jude pointed at the television. "Something terrible just happened. The police shot that man for nothing. The same way they shot Stephen for nothing, and now he is being tormented forever."

Isaac held out his hand to Nina and Jude. He led them in prayer, "Lord Jesus, we thank You for all that You have done for this family. We give You praise for keeping us safe. But there are many in this world who are not safe, and are dying needless deaths. Give us direction Lord. Show us what to do… where to go… who to help. Send the one who is destined to help our people in times like these."

"Amen, in Jesus name we pray," Nina finished for Isaac, as it became obvious to her that he was getting weak again.

Isaac laid his head back on the pillow and then turned to Jude. "I am sorry about what happened to Stephen. Your mom and I could tell that you were in bad shape after his death. Have you been able to make peace with God yet?"

To his father everything was a spiritual issue. Why couldn't Jude just be mad, without being mad at God? But in truth, Jude was angry with God, especially after that nightmare he experienced the other night. Ringing his hands, he confessed, "I need to talk to you about something."

"I don't like the look in your eyes, Jude. You're angry so I think this conversation my need to wait until your father is a bit healthier," Nina admonished.

But Isaac shook his head. "We can't be like that Nina. I don't know how much time I have left and Jude and I have unfinished business."

"Don't talk like that." The frustration was showing on Nina's face.

"You're only 85 years old, Dad. Plenty of people have lived longer."

"And I am grateful for every next day that God sends, because I truly never expected to live this long.

The way I lived my life, I thought I'd be dead before forty."

"But you didn't die," Nina reminded him. "You beat the odds and Our God is going to help you beat this too. You and I will go in the rapture, remember?"

"Yeah, baby. That's our plan." Isaac smiled at his wife, still the most beautiful woman, inside and out, that he'd ever met. "Now let me talk to our son."

Nina patted his hand and then stepped back and sat down.

Isaac turned back to Jude. "Say what's on your mind, Son."

"I don't want to upset you, but I really need answers. Remember how I told you about my trip to Hell a few years ago?"

"I remember."

"You told me that it probably wasn't what I thought, and that I was only imagining the trip because of the information you had given me about your ordeal."

"Yes, but I also told you to pray and ask for the Lord to help you if you experienced it again."

"I did that, and those demons would leave me alone. But this last trip was different. Just as I was about to get beat down again, Truth showed up. I was afraid of him at first, but He was the only One who could get those demons off of me. So, I followed Him. He took me to the Fun Room."

Hearing that, Isaac's eyes filled with tears."

"Stephen was there and he was being tortured. Truth told me that would happen over and over again."

With anguish showing on his face, Isaac told him. "I know the Fun Room well. My brother resides in there, and there hasn't been a day that God opens my eyes that I haven't begged for that to change."

"Truth acted like it was my fault. Like I wasn't doing something I'm supposed to be doing. But I don't know what I'm supposed to do, and I can't get the image of Stephen being pulled apart out of my mind. If I could do anything to help him, I'd do it in a minute."

Sorrow filled Isaac's eyes, as he told his son, "You can't help Stephen. It's over for him."

"Then what's the point, Dad? Why did I have to see him in that Fun Room if I can't do anything about it?"

"I don't know for sure what God wants from you. But, with me, I was able to take my heartache and turn it into my life's mission. So all I can tell you is seek the Lord, my son. I caused many untimely deaths, but I have also helped many, many people lift up their eyes in Heaven, and that brings me peace."

~~~~

Marissa expected to see Jude at the hospital the other day, but she didn't expect her heart to betray her. As she hid under the covers, not wanting to get out of bed, Marissa realized that she was still in love with Jude. "I gave him back to You Lord. All I asked, was for You to give me back my heart."

For the last few years Marissa thought she had reclaimed her heart from Jude. She had even dated Elder Lou. She enjoyed hanging out with Lou and getting to know him. Marissa had hoped that she and Lou might be able to build a life together, because they shared the same values. But once they stopped talking about the Bible, she and Lou had nothing else in common.

Lou didn't believe that a woman should work outside the home, but Marissa hadn't gone to college so she could sit at home, making meals and keeping the house spotless. No, Marissa would rather have a successful and fulfilling career, than dust or mop the kitchen floor. She called Mighty Maids for the house cleaning and kept it moving.

Lou didn't believe women should preach, but Marissa was now taking classes for her ministry license. When Lou told her that women should be silent in church, so they could listen and take notes on how to keep their husband happy, that's when she knew that they were not going to work.

Marissa had been relieved when Lou started dating Stacey Mills. She felt bad for Stacey, but Lou stopped calling, and stopping by her house asking if they could get back together. Lou left her alone all together, and had even started telling people that she was too progressive for his liking.

Even though dating Lou had been a mistake, he had provided a very necessary distraction from her constant thoughts about Jude. Lou had also provided a distraction from the thoughts of missing out on marriage and children, and Marissa desperately wanted children. Her heart still yearned for the baby that she lost when she was just a teenager, hanging out with the wrong crowd and getting involved with the wrong man.

Tony Jones had been the handsome bad boy in her neighborhood, and Marissa had fallen for him before she figured out that he wasn't an honorable kind of guy. When she told Tony that she was pregnant, he went around the neighborhood telling everyone that he was not the father and that she had slept around. But Marissa wasn't that kind of girl. She had been so depressed during that time in her life, that she had even contemplated suicide. But then Jude knocked on her door, and invited her to a tent revival.

Marissa had never told Jude that she had been thinking about taking the entire bottle of her mother's sleeping pills. He never knew that he had helped to save her life that day. Because even though she had agreed to come to the revival, she told herself that she would just take the pills once she came back home. But Pastor Isaac was on fire for the Lord that day. He preached about the love of God... something that Marissa hadn't felt much of until that day.

She accepted Christ into her life, and from that day to this, Marissa had never been so low that she wanted to kill herself; not even when she laid in the hospital touching her empty stomach with the knowledge that her baby had died.

Jude had been there for her during those terrible days. They made so many promises to each other back then. They were going to love each other forever, just as they loved God. She and Jude had promised to come back home after college and start their own ministry. It was going to be bigger than Pastor Isaac's ministry. But none of that happened, because when Jude finally came back for her, it was only because of their love... Jude no longer cared about ministry or the love of God they had once had in common.

She loved him and wanted nothing more than to be with him forever, but the man who had returned to her was almost nothing like the boy who'd left. Marissa found herself wondering if Jude would have been better off if he had stayed home and worked in the ministry as Pastor Isaac had wanted him to do. But Nina had wanted Jude to experience college, just as Donavan and Iona had done. "Lord, please help me get through these few days that Jude will be back in town."

Marissa crawled out of bed and jumped into the shower. She had a lunch date that she couldn't miss just because she was heart sick today. Actually, it wasn't a date, more like a ministry appointment. Tony Jones, the guy who had gotten her pregnant and then pretended that he wasn't the father, was back in town. He had spent the last ten years in prison and now that he was out, he wanted to talk to her.

Marissa wanted to talk to him also. She needed to know if he had received any of the letters that she sent him through the years.

10

Jude needed to clear his mind. He left the hospital and headed to one of the best steak places in town. It wasn't a 5-star restaurant, but rather a little mom and pop place that he and Marissa used to eat at all the time that summer before they left for college. He took the same booth that he and Marissa used to sit at while they gazed into each other's eyes, making promises for the future.

"I don't need a menu," he told the waitress. "I'll take the prime rib, loaded potato and the veggie mix."

"What you know about our veggie mix?" the waitress asked, grinning at him.

"I used to live here. This restaurant holds some special memories for me, so of course I know that the veggie mix here is the best in the city."

"Well, all right then. I'll make sure that they put some extra veggies on your plate."

As the waitress walked away, Jude leaned his head against the headrest of his booth. His eyes focused on the seat across from him... the one Marissa used to sit in, and his mind drifted back to their last meal together.

He was holding her hand and gazing into her eyes. Jude still saw so much sadness in those eyes and he wanted desperately to remove the pain. "I wish I could put a smile on your face today."

"You put a smile on my face every day, Ikee. If you hadn't come into my life when you did... I don't even like to think where I would be."

"Sometimes I wish we had met a little later, after that sorted mess with Calvin Jones had been taken care of, then you wouldn't have been at that revival and wouldn't have gotten hurt or lost the baby."

"You probably wouldn't have met me at all if you hadn't knocked on my door that day."

His eyebrow lifted, as a curious expression crossed his face. "What's that supposed to mean?"

Marissa shook her head. "Nothing... just saying. We need to trust God's timing. I believe God sent you to my door the exact day and time you arrived. And I thank you for allowing God to direct you. I'm honored that a man of God like you, would care so much about me."

Jude had been flattered at Marissa's words back then, but years later he realized that Marissa hadn't just been flattering him. She truly wanted a man of God in her life; and rejected him out right when he tried to rekindle their relationship, because she no longer saw him as a man of God.

His food arrived and as he lifted his head to thank the waitress, Jude watched Marissa and some thug-life dude being seated on the other side of the restaurant.

~~~~

Marissa didn't feel comfortable giving Tony her address so she agreed to meet him at the restaurant. She pulled up and got out of her car. It wasn't until she stood in front of the door that she remembered. Standing there she was struck by the fact that she had forgotten about this restaurant. This place had once been she and Jude's favorite place to eat. But Marissa hadn't been back here in years. When Tony asked to meet her here, it hadn't clicked. But now that memories were flooding her very being, Marissa wanted to get back in her car and get as far away from this place as possible.

"Why are you staring at the door like that?"

Marissa swung around. Tony was walking over to her. He had cornrows in his head, baggy jeans and a well-worn t-shirt on. Tony looked nothing like the kind of man that she would date, and it allowed Marissa to see just how far God had brought her. "I was just thinking about something. How are you doing?"

Tony smiled at her, and Marissa saw actual joy in his eyes. "That's why I asked you to lunch. I want to tell you what has happened to me since we broke up."

Marissa remembered things a bit differently. They couldn't have broken up, because Tony went around town telling anyone who would listen that she was never his woman and that she slept around anyway. But she would let him have it his way. "I'm starving so let's go on in. You can tell me all about it after we order our food."

They took a seat at a table on the opposite side of the room than the booth she and Jude used to sit at. Marissa's back was to the booth on the other side of the room, because she didn't want to find herself gazing toward it, remembering the past when she should be paying attention to Tony.

They ordered their meal and then Tony touched Marissa's hand. She was about to pull her hand out of his grasp, but then he said, "Before we talk, I want to apologize to you about the baby."

She shook her head. "It was a long time ago. We were both kids."

"Don't excuse my actions, Marissa. We might have been kids, but I had no right to treat you the way I did. Especially since I knew the baby you carried was mine."

She nodded. "Thank you for saying that."

He released her hand and leaned back in his seat. "Look at you now... looking all refined. Like you some Corporate America CEO or something."

Maybe she shouldn't have worn her tan pants suit. It was one of the most business like suits in her closet, but she didn't want to wear anything that might encourage Tony's advances. "I'm hardly a CEO. I manage a youth program that's owned by the church I attend."

"Listen at you... manager."

Tony looked impressed, but Marissa wasn't bragging. This was just her life, and in truth, she didn't think she was doing enough.

"I'm proud of you, Marissa. But I didn't ask you to lunch to tell you that."

"So, what is it that you want me to know?"

~~~

Jude bit down on his lip as he watched that thug put his hands on Marissa. She didn't move her hand away, almost as if she was enjoying the advances of this thug. The scene playing out before him was galling because this dude didn't look like he knew the first thing about God. But here Marissa was, on a date with this guy, when she wouldn't even walk down the street with him.

Jude didn't like this at all. But, some part of him couldn't believe that Marissa wanted some thug-life guy. She and Lou may have broken up, but Lou was as straight laced as they came... too straight as far as Jude was concerned, so how could Marissa have gone from Lou the church elder, to thug-life? He didn't know what was going on, but he was going to get to the bottom of it. He lifted a hand, signaling the waitress. When she arrived at his table, he said, "Can I get the bill?"

"You don't like your food? You've barely touched it."

"It's good. I'll have to finish it later though. So can I get a to-go box as well?"

The waitress boxed Jude's food as he paid the bill. He then got out of his seat and walked over to where Marissa was as if he had been invited. "Well look who's here?" Jude rudely interrupted their conversation, not even caring that the dude she was with was in mid-sentence. Because what he really wanted to know was how in the world she could bring some other dude to the place he took her on their first and last dates.

Marissa turned her head and glanced up at him. "Hey Jude. How is Pastor Isaac doing?"

"He's resting."

Marissa smiled as if waiting for Jude to provide further information. When none came but he kept standing there, she turned to Tony and said, "Tony, I don't know if you remember Jude. We used to call him Ikee back in the day. He's Pastor Isaac Walker's son."

Oh, so that's all he was, huh? At one time Jude was much more than Pastor Walker's son to Marissa. But she must have blocked that out of her mind.

"I know about Pastor Walker. All my brother Calvin talked about was how he hated him. Calvin blamed Pastor Walker for the life sentence he received. It never even occurred to Calvin to apologize to me for leaving that explosive at Pastor Walker's revival, and then causing you to lose our baby."

Jude's mouth dropped. He pointed at the guy. "This is Tony Jones?"

Marissa looked from one side of the restaurant to the other. "Why are you yelling?"

"I'm not yelling," Jude said, still yelling. He then took a deep breath and brought his voice down. "I just don't understand why you're at *our* restaurant with this dude."

"This isn't our restaurant, Jude. Anybody can eat here. And you are being rude to Tony. So, please stop."

Tony waved a hand. "Look man, I'm not trying to put the move on Marissa. I invited her to lunch so I could thank her, that's all."

Jude felt like a fool standing there angry when he had no right to be angry. But he couldn't stop himself from feeling the way he felt.

"You don't owe him an explanation, Tony."

But Tony took another approach. "Have a seat with us, man. I don't mind if you hear what I have to say to her."

"Do you mind, Marissa?" Jude waited for her to answer.

Sighing, Marissa told him, "I don't mind you sitting with us." But she gave him a look that said, 'sit somewhere else'.

Grinning at her, Jude told Tony. "Thanks for the invitation. I believe I will join you." He sat down. Opened his container, borrowed Marissa's knife to cut his steak as he said, "Go ahead with what you were saying, Tony."

Marissa gave him the evil eye, but Jude ignored it.

"I never wrote you back when I was in prison. But I wanted you to know that I got your letters."

"Letters?" Jude's eyebrow lifted as he pointedly glanced at Marissa while swiping her fork.

The waitress brought Marissa and Tony's food and Marissa said, "Can I have some more silverware please."

"Sure, I'll be right back with it."

As the waitress handed Marissa the silverware, she bowed her head and prayed over their food and then said to Tony, "I wondered if you ever received my letters."

"I did and I came here today to tell you that I actually laughed at your first letter, and threw it away."

Marissa laughed. "I thought you might have. That's why I sent you a few more after that first one."

"I'm glad that you did."

Jude looked back and forth, trying to figure out what was going on. Why on earth was Marissa writing letters to prisoners when she wouldn't even go out on a date with him?

"I didn't throw away the second one, but I didn't open it until after the third one came. I said to myself... this girl isn't going to stop. So I opened the third letter and read it. When you described how God had changed your life and how you had graduated from college... and then you wrote that you forgave me for how I acted when you got pregnant, I have to tell you, I broke down right there in my cell and cried.

"I didn't even know that I needed to be forgiven for that. I knew that you had lost the baby and that my brother had a hand in that, but I hadn't really thought much about it until you started writing me about the love of God. By the time I opened the second letter and read how you described the way I could be forgiven for my sins, that was the day that my life changed."

Marissa was cheesing from ear to ear, she put her fork down and touched Tony's hand. "Are you saying what I think you're saying?"

Tony nodded. "I'm saved."

11

"That was surprising," Jude said to Marissa as they stood outside the restaurant.

"What are you talking about?" Marissa was unhappy with Jude's actions and she wasn't about to let him off the hook.

"I came over to your table because I couldn't believe that you were out to lunch with a guy like that, especially after you turned me down."

"Everything is not about you, Jude." She threw up her hands, grunted and stomped off to her car.

"Hey wait a minute." Jude rushed over to her. He grabbed her arm to stop her from opening her car door. "Why are you so upset with me? I'm just saying that Tony surprised me. That's all."

"Well, I didn't like your attitude. You didn't have to treat him like that. I'm surprised that he felt comfortable enough to ask for help with finding a job."

"I'm glad he did ask, I still have some connections in this city and I'm going to see about getting him a job."

That calmed her. Marissa relaxed a bit. "Thank you. I appreciate your doing that. Tony has given his life to Christ, all he needs is a break to help him turn his life around."

Jude leaned against Marissa's car as he studied her. "You're really something, you know that?"

"I'm just Marissa Allen, nothing more, nothing less."

"Yeah, but you didn't have to forgive Tony for what he did to you back in the day. And you certainly didn't have to send him multiple letters urging him to accept the Lord in his life. Sounds like something my mother would have done."

Marissa smiled. "Who do you think advised me to write Tony?"

Jude laughed. "My mother couldn't stand you when I first introduced you to her. Now all of a sudden the two of you are like best friends."

Marissa elbowed Jude. "She no longer has to worry about me stealing her little boy away, so we have a much better relationship now."

"All you had to do was break up with her son, huh?"

"I didn't break up with you, Jude. You rarely called me once we finished college. You went on with your life, leaving me back here waiting on you to come home."

"Oh but I did come home. And that's when you accused me of changing and not having the same love for God that I once had. You acted like you were so much better than me and I just didn't want to deal with that."

She remembered the day Jude had come home. It was the last time he'd been home for Thanksgiving. Marissa had been excited to see him and had prayed that he was ready to come home and work in the ministry with her.

But Jude wasn't interested in the ministry anymore. He stood in front of her bragging about how much money he was making and how wonderful life was going for him. He wanted nothing to do with the ministry he once loved being a part of. He did, however, want Marissa to be a part of his world. But Marissa couldn't be a part of a world that didn't include the God that she served.

The hardest thing she ever had to do was to tell Jude that she wouldn't move to California with him, and that she couldn't even think about going out with him again until he rededicated his life to Christ.

"I wish things had turned out differently for us, Jude, I really do."

Jude's eyes filled with sorrow, then he shaded them as he pulled himself off of her car and shoved his hands in his pocket. "I get it. I'm just not the guy for you."

That's what she kept telling herself. But as he stood there looking so gorgeous and so vulnerable all she wanted to do was put her arms around him and tell him how much she still loved him. But God had not released her to love Jude, so she had to keep that information to herself. Pulling her keys out of her purse, she asked him, "Will I see you at the hospital this evening?"

"I'm sure I'll be there."

"Well, all right then. See you later." She opened her car door, got in and locked the door even before turning on the car. Because if Jude opened her door and attempted to explain himself one more time, she might just kiss him. It was truly a good feeling to be loved. And Marissa believed that Jude loved her. She never doubted his words on that for a minute.

From the moment they met, Jude had been the one for her. But Jude was also the one who helped introduce her to Christ. When they were teenagers, she and Jude spent many hours studying the word and she thought that their faith was growing stronger. But something changed Jude. So, even though Marissa loved him just as much as he loved her, if not more, she would not marry a man who had turned his back on the very same God she vowed to love and serve until the day she died.

~~~~

When Jude got back to the hospital, Keith was seated next to his father's bed, lounging in the reclining chair. Keith had the Bible in his hand and he was reading out of Revelations as Jude sat down on the opposite side of his father's bed.

After these things I looked, and behold, a great multitude which no one could number, of all nations, tribes, peoples, and tongues, standing before the throne and before the Lamb, clothed with white robes, with palm branches in their hands, and crying out with a loud voice, saying, "Salvation belongs to our God who sits on the throne, and to the Lamb!" All the angels stood around the throne and the elders and the four living creatures, and fell on their faces before the throne and worshiped God, saying: "Amen! Blessing and glory and wisdom, thanksgiving and honor and power and might, Be to our God forever and ever. Amen."

*Then one of the elders answered, saying to me,
"Who are these arrayed in white robes, and where did
they come from?"*

And I said to him, "Sir, you know."

*So he said to me, "These are the ones who come
out of the great tribulation, and washed their robes
and made them white in the blood of the Lamb.
Therefore they are before the throne of God, and
serve Him day and night in His temple. And He who
sits on the throne will dwell among them. They shall
neither hunger anymore nor thirst anymore; the sun
shall not strike them, nor any heat; for the Lamb who
is in the midst of the throne will shepherd them and
lead them to living fountains of waters. And God will
wipe away every tear from their eyes."*

As Keith put the Bible down, Isaac turned to his
old friend and said, "That's what we want, right? To
be counted in that number who goes during the Great
Tribulation."

"Man, what you talking 'bout? You must have
forgotten what we came out of. As far as I'm
concerned, you and me, we done been through a
tribulation already. So, when God wants to take me
and Cynda out of here, even though the kids will miss
us, I still say, I'm ready my friend."

"Hold up, Uncle Keith. You can't be talking like that while my Dad is trying to recover. If he wants to go in the rapture, then I'm fine with that." Jude didn't like the sound of this. He didn't want anyone encouraging his dad to drop the mic and kick up dirt. His mom and dad had him late in life, so they owed it to him to hang around a little while longer.

"Don't worry son, I'm not going nowhere until God says it's time."

"What y'all need to do is get back on the road with those street revivals. Remember how much fun that was?" Jude asked.

Keith rubbed his knees. "I wish I could, but these old knees won't allow me to do too much travel these days."

Isaac laughed at that. "I'll take your knees for my aching back any day."

"Don't nobody won't that bad back of yours. You messed it up, so you're stuck with it," Keith told his buddy.

"I don't like the way y'all sound. Before I left for college, both of y'all were running circles around me, now look at you."

"We're old, son. Just as the Bible says, 'to everything there is a season'. But I'll tell you, I always thought that you would come back home and take over for me and Keith."

"Me?" Jude put a hand to his chest. "Why not Donavan?"

"Donavan has taken over as the head pastor at the church. He has to concentrate his efforts on our members."

That bit of information was news to Jude. "When did Donavan take over as head pastor? And why didn't anyone tell me?"

Isaac eyed his son a moment before responding. "My back has been giving me trouble for a few years now. Donavan has steadily been taking on more responsibility and although it hasn't been announced yet, your mother and I thought it best to let him take over as senior pastor while I serve more of an advisory role."

"So you're not preaching anymore either?" Jude couldn't believe this. It seemed to him that he had turned his back for just a moment and everything had changed.

"Of course I'm still preaching. I'm going to be telling folks about my savior until they put me in that pine box. I might be moving a little slower these days, but ain't nothing changed but the date."

Jude wanted off this subject like he wanted to breathe. So, he told them. "I met this guy at lunch today. He gave his life to God while in prison."

"Sounds like my story. Did I ever tell you how God got my attention when I was in prison?"

"That was when you took your first trip to Hell, right?" Jude wished he could forget that. Maybe if his father had never told him about those terrible nightmares that plagued him... maybe, just maybe Jude wouldn't be going through the same thing now.

"Yes, but it was more than that. Because I was about to kill a man when God allowed me to see what death really meant to those who died before receiving Christ in their lives. It made me realize that I didn't have the right to take a life. It wasn't long after that that I got on my knees and prayed for God to change my life. The funny thing is, I still remember it as if it just happened."

"The reason I brought him up is that he's looking for a job so he can stay on the right path. Do either of you know something that I might be able to point him to?"

"We have a program at the church that helps ex-convicts with felonies on their record start their own business," Nina said as she walked into the room.

Jude swung around to greet his mother. "When did you get here?"

"I've been here a little while, I was standing at the door listening to you all for a minute."

"Well thanks for the idea, but I doubt that Tony has any money to start his own business."

Nina shook her head. "He doesn't need the money. Once he finishes the program, we will loan him the money to start the business."

"That's perfect, Mom." Jude got out of his seat and kissed Nina on the cheek. "Let me go tell Tony, and see if he wants to take part in the program."

Keith stood up. "I'll come with you because I can explain more about the program since I have mentored several ex-cons through the program."

~~~~

Once Jude and Keith left, Nina sat down next to her husband. The look on her face was downright discouraging. She looked as if she wanted to cry.

"I don't like that look," Isaac told her.

"Well, I can't help it. I'm not feeling very good right now."

"Do you want to talk about it?"

She nodded. "I feel like I owe you an apology."

"What? No."

"Hear me out, my love. I was wrong and I owe it to you to admit that. Because you never wanted Jude to go to college. You and I got into arguments about this and you let me win. So we sent Jude off to college, believing that once educated he would come back and take over the evangelistic part of the ministry.

"I think that it has always bothered me that I got pregnant with Donavan and then dropped out of college, never to return. Therefore, I made sure that Donavan, Iona and Jude made their education a priority. But maybe God never intended for Jude to go to college. He certainly never wanted to go; all that boy wanted back then was to stay home and help you with those revivals."

"I get all of that," Isaac said, then added, "But why are you so sad? Aren't you a praying woman?"

Nina's eyes filled as she held out her hands to Isaac. "Will you pray with me?"

12

"Where'd you meet this guy?" Keith asked as they drove down the street, headed to the west side of town.

Jude didn't want to admit this, but he couldn't lie to his Uncle Keith, not about something so innocuous. "He's an old friend of Marissa's. I met him at lunch."

"You and Marissa went to lunch today?" Keith words sounded hopeful.

Jude shook his head. "Nothing like that. We both happened to be eating at the same restaurant and I joined her and Tony for lunch." Jude side-eyed Keith.

Keith was grinning as he said, "You cut in on the girl's lunch? Couldn't stand that she was out with someone else, huh?"

"I'll admit it. I was ready to go heads up with the guy when I saw him sitting with Marissa. But when I sat down with them, I realized that he was for real.

Tony just needs a break and I'm glad that the church will be able to help him with that."

"You're doing a good thing, Jude. But why don't you just call him? Why are we driving all the way to his house?"

"At lunch today, Tony told us that his cell phone is off right now. He gave me his address if anything came up."

They pulled up in front of the housing project that Tony lived in and got out of the car. The apartment was in one of the poorest areas of the city, so Jude knew that Tony was seriously hurting for money if he stayed here. This knowledge made him feel small at how angry he had been at Tony, a man he didn't even know just because he had been sitting with Marissa. If he hadn't sat down with them he never would have known that Tony was a man who was on the verge of changing his life, and just needed someone to care enough to lend a helping hand.

People were hanging out on the streets selling and buying drugs, but Tony wasn't out there trying to earn some quick cash to pay his cell phone bill. When Jude knocked on the door, and Tony answered, he had an application in his hand.

"Hey man, what's up?" Tony asked.

"I've got some good news for you," Jude said.

Tony opened the door wider. "Come on in. I need some good news in my life right now."

"This is my Uncle Keith," Jude said as they stepped into the living room.

Tony took a bunch of newspapers off of the sofa and Keith and Jude sat down. "What this good news?"

"I'll let my uncle tell you since he works with the program."

Keith cleared his throat, leaned forward. "Jude told me and his father about your job situation. And we came here to tell you about a program we have at the church. As I'm sure you know, anyone with a felony on their record will have a hard time getting a decent job."

"Tell me about it." Tony lifted up the newspapers he had just removed from the sofa. "I have called so many companies trying to get my foot in the door and nobody wants to hear from me. And I've probably got more experience than the guys they're giving the job to... I spent ten years in the joint learning auto body and I'm good at it."

"I'm glad to know that you've already developed a skill," Keith told him. "The program we have doesn't only help with developing skills, we also teach you how to write a business plan. Then we take it a step further by loaning our candidates the money needed to start their business once the business plan has been completed and a building or location has been pinpointed."

Tony flopped down in the chair across from the sofa. "I've never heard about a church doing anything like that for people."

"I'm an ex-con and so is Isaac, so we've been working to help people like us for many years," Keith told him.

"And you're going to help me?" Tony sounded skeptical, like he couldn't believe that something good was coming his way.

"You can start with the program on Monday if you like. Oh, and we also pay out a small stipend for each week your in the program. The money helps you pay your bills and put enough gas in your car so you can make it to the church each week."

"You don't need to convince me. I'm in." Tony shook both Keith and Jude's hands and thanked them. "If you all can help me start my business this means that I can ask my girl to marry me."

"Your girl?" Jude questioned.

Laughing, Tony lifted a hand. "Easy Jude. I'm not talking about Marissa. One of my girls from back in the day stayed in contact with me while I was locked up. She was there for me and now I want to man up and be there for her."

"I didn't mean to imply anything," Jude said feeling embarrassed at how fast he jumped on Tony's words.

"It's not a problem man. But you might want to talk to Marissa about how you feel. It was written all over your face at lunch."

She knows and she doesn't care, Jude wanted to tell him. But instead said, "We've got to go. I hope the program works out for you."

~~~~

Jude left Tony's place feeling as if he'd done a good deed, something he used to do on the regular when he worked in the ministry with his father. But these days, he didn't have time for good deeds, when he was always trying to cover his back to keep from getting stabbed in it by business partners and by other developers trying to steal their app and make money off of it.

13

Just as things seemed to be turning around, the storm came and turned everything upside down. Jude was in his father's office at the church, getting ready to go into the sanctuary and sit with his mother, when his cell phone rang. He picked up and that familiar voice shouted, "Did you see the news?"

"Marissa? Is that you?" Jude asked, her voice sounded strange, as if she'd been crying.

"It's me, Jude. Are you watching the news?"

"No, I'm in my dad's office at the church."

"Turn on the television, please."

"Are you crying?" he asked as he picked the remote off the desk and hit the power button. Once it was on, he changed it to the channel she commanded.

"It's Tony," She sniffed and then blew her nose. "The police shot him last night."

"What?" was his only response as he turned his attention to the television? A cell phone video had just been released and it showed the officer holding Tony against his car. The officer leaned in, whispered something in Tony's ear, then Tony broke free and tried to run. But then the officer shot him in the back.

That same officer then opened the trunk of his car, pulled a gun out, walked over to Tony and placed the gun on the ground next to him. The officer was then heard calling the encounter in to dispatch. But the officer claimed that Tony held up a gun, getting ready to shoot at him so he fired his weapon.

"He murdered Tony," Marissa yelled into the phone.

"I'm seeing it, but I can't believe my eyes. Is this for real?"

"This is the second time this is being shown. I watched it the first time, and they said Tony died out there. I've been trying to get ready for church, but I haven't been able to stop crying."

"You're too upset to drive. Finish getting dressed. I'll be there to get you." He hung up the phone, grabbed his keys off the desk and headed out of the back door. His mother would wonder where he was, but he would explain once he returned.

He arrived at Marissa's place within fifteen minutes. As she opened the door Jude noticed that she was fully dressed with no make-up on her face. As he stepped into the living room Marissa fell in his arms and cried so much that his heart broke for her.

Jude wrapped his arms around her. "I'm sorry, Marissa. I'm really sorry." And the thing about it was, Jude truly felt awful about what happened to Tony. He had turned out to be a good guy. Tony didn't deserve what happened to him, just like Stephen didn't deserve to get shot by the police, nor that guy with his hands up next to his car. Something was wicked in this earth and something needed to be done about it.

"I feel so helpless," Marissa confessed as she pulled herself out of Jude's embrace.

Jude didn't say anything because he felt the same way. He wanted to smash something, but didn't know how tearing up the world would bring Tony back, so he could attend the program at the church and get the money needed to start his own business.

But then Jude said something that he hadn't thought to do in many years. "Do you think we should pray?"

Marissa wiped some of the tears from her face as she stared up at Jude, as if amazed by his comment.

"I mean," Jude continued. "Not for Tony. Thanks to you we both know that he is in heaven, but for all the people that his death will affect. What we saw on

TV today was nothing short of murder, and I just..."
Jude searched for the words.

Marissa took his hands. "Yes, we should pray."
And so they did.

By the time they arrived at the church Donavan was already behind the pulpit preaching his heart out about an unthankful world and a God who deserves all the thanks and praise. "You see my friends," Donavan was saying, "Timothy was on to something when he tried to tell us how this world would be. Open your Bibles to 1 Timothy Chapter 3 and let's read." He waited a few moments as pages began turning then he read:

But know this, that in the last days perilous times will come: For men will be lovers of themselves, lovers of money, boasters, proud, blasphemers, disobedient to parents, unthankful, unholy, unloving, unforgiving, slanderers, without self-control, brutal, despisers of good, traitors, headstrong, haughty, lovers of pleasure rather than lovers of God, having a form of godliness but denying its power. And from such people turn away!

Every word Donavan read hit Jude like a punch in the gut... because it was just like the prophet told King David, after King David had listened to a story about a rich man who had everything, yet stole the one and only thing a poor man had. When David became angry at the gall that a human being would do such a thing, the prophet then informed him, "You Are the man." It was one of David's lowest moments as king, when he had to come to terms with the fact that he had murdered Bathsheba's husband, and claimed her to be his wife even though he already had several wives.

I am the man, Jude said to himself. God had been good to him. Everything his hands touched succeeded. But did Jude ever turn back and thank the Lord for that? No, instead he became a lover of money, unholy, unthankful, and proud. His family had been trying to get him to see the errors of his ways for the past few years. They could plainly see that Jude had been led astray by the allure of riches, but he hadn't listened to them, nor had he listened to Micah.

Jude hadn't even been listening when Marissa no longer wanted to be a part of his world. But the words his brother had just read were powerful, because it finally showed him why Marissa wanted nothing to do with him… *and from such people turn away.*

He believed that Marissa had been in love with him, just as he was with her. But Marissa had chosen to follow after God while Jude followed after the cares of this world... a*nd from such people turn away*.

As the altar call was going forward, Jude wanted to run to the altar and throw himself at the feet of Jesus to discover if there was any mercy for his sins. But just as he was contemplating what to do and whether he could truly make a change in his life, Elder Lou tapped his mom on the shoulder and beckoned her to follow him. His mom grabbed his hand and pulled him with her.

Once they were standing outside of Isaac's office, Lou informed them, "The Mayor is on hold. He is requesting help from our leadership."

"Help with what?" Nina asked as she opened the door to Isaac's office.

"The people are rioting in the street. They've overturned cars, busted out windows of businesses and started looting. Two of them have already been killed," Lou told her.

"Am I missing something? What's going on?" Nina looked from Lou to Jude waiting for an answer.

Jude stepped forward. "Tony Jones, the guy Keith and I enrolled into the entrepreneur program, was murdered by the police last night."

Nina lifted a hand, halting her son. "That's a serious accusation. Before we blame the police for shooting another black man, don't you think we should get the facts first?"

"A cell phone video was released this morning, Mama. The cop shot Tony in the back as he was running away from him and then he planted a gun on him."

"Oh Good Lord. I sure wish your daddy was here." Shaking her head, she picked up the phone and spoke with the mayor. "Hello Randall, I hear things aren't going so well." Nina held the phone and listened for a few minutes, then she told him, "My husband is in the hospital but I'll see what we can do."

When she hung up, Nina turned back to Jude and Lou. "The mayor is looking for some leadership, and with your father being in the hospital and Donavan needed here, I'm going to need you."

Jude turned from side to side and then asked, "Who, Lou?"

Nina smiled at her son. "I'd like Lou to go, but he is needed here at the church. Donavan and the other men are getting ready to clear out the sanctuary once again so that we can finish our shipment of food to Haiti. But you are Isaac Judah Walker, and the mayor needs a Walker out there doing what you're father normally would have done."

"This sounds like something Donavan should be handling," Jude urged. His mother had lost her mind. He hadn't been a part of the family business in years, this wasn't who he was anymore. How could he speak for his father when he wasn't even sure how he felt about some of the things he was feeling right now?

Nina shook her head. "I just told you… Donavan has work to do at the church."

Jude turned away from his mother, then turned back toward her. "How can I do this, Mama? I'm not apart of this ministry anymore."

"It's in your blood baby. You were born for this moment. Now, this city needs you. The people are rioting and looting. The people need a leader and I know you don't want to disappoint your dad."

That was a low blow and it came from his sweet and loving mother. A woman who strived to bring light into the world and help others feel good about who God made them to be. She was now, making him feel lousy about the man he had become. "I'll go. But if I end up rioting with the crowd rather than calming them down, blame yourself for not sending someone more qualified for this moment."

"I have faith in you. Go with God, Son."

Jude left the office and then went to the entry door of the sanctuary. Marissa looked up to see him standing there. He signaled for her. Marissa met in the hallway. "What's going on? Why did you leave the service?"

"There's rioting and looting going on downtown. I have to go and try to calm the situation. So, I want you to ride home with my Mom."

"I'm going with you."

"I don't think it's safe. You should stay here."

Marissa shook her head. "I saw that video this morning. The people are angry so this could be a dangerous situation."

"Exactly why I don't want you to go." Jude started walking away from Marissa.

She grabbed hold of his arm and said, "I'm going and that's it."

14

When they reached the mayor in the downtown area, Jude watched as the police tried to restore order to people that were just sick and tired of being sick and tired. Jude felt their pain. When Stephen had been killed by the police for simply trying to remove his seat belt during a traffic stop, Jude had smashed his fist in his sixty inch flat screen TV. He'd moped around the house, refusing to enjoy life, and demanded answers that never came. So he understood the anger these people felt.

The anger boiled deeper in him because Tony didn't deserve to die like that. He was a decent man who was trying to turn his life around. What right did that cop have to shoot him like that? What right did any of these cops have to shoot to kill black men as if they were target practice?

The mayor handed Jude a bullhorn. He said, "We've got to do something to stop this. It will cost tens of millions of dollars to repair all the damage."

"You sent for us because you're worried about property damage?" Jude was so incensed with anger that he was about to take that bullhorn and go bust out a window or two himself. But then Marissa lightly touched his arm and began singing praises to God.

"Our God is greater... our God is stronger... our God... our God."

Her touch and the sound of her voice calmed him. He began thinking about his father and how Pastor Walker would give his life for these angry kids. He would go through the fire so that one of these wounded and hurting souls would come to know and understand that God loves them, and that He never intended for life to be like this.

The mayor then said, "It's not just about the property. They want to protest, but they are rioting instead. Two men have already been killed and I don't want these cops to get trigger happy again, do you?

Jude shook his head.

The mayor pressed the bullhorn toward Jude again. "Then, please, help me calm these people down."

As Jude grabbed hold of the bullhorn he closed his eyes and imagined himself at one of his father's street revivals. His dad was an awesome man of God and when he spoke it was with power and authority. Jude didn't know if he had it in him to be like his dad, but for the people's sake he was bound and determined to try. Marissa was standing behind him and he could hear her quietly praying. She was a warrior for God and he was grateful that she bum rushed her way into his car. Her prayer and praise was building him up.

"Listen, listen to me for a moment." People were chanting Black Lives Matter and angrily thrusting signs in the air that read, "Stop Killing Us"

"I know you're angry. So am I. You want to protest this senseless killing and so do I. I want to come down there and pick up one of those signs and shove it in the face of every police officer who looks at us and does not see a human being who has worth to the community and to their family."

His voice filled with anger as he said, "I want to shout on a mountain top, Black Lives Matter, because they do." But then he quieted as he added. "I know how you feel and you have a right to feel this way. But we don't have a right to tear this city down… a city that my father loves and has worked diligently for the last thirty some years to rebuild after the drug epidemic tried to destroy it.

"Many of you are too young to remember what this city was like before my father, Pastor Isaac Walker gave his life to the Lord and started pulling one person after the next out of darkness, but I'm telling you that things were really bad here back then. Don't let your anger destroy the progress that has been made in this city... your community... your homes."

"We're tired of taking this. Somebody needs to pay," one of the men yelled out.

"I agree with you," Jude shouted back. "That officer who shot Tony Jones needs to be prosecuted. But the people who own these stores, and who've had their windows bust out, they don't need to pay."

"Then what are we supposed to do?" A woman who looked as if she'd cried many tears shouted.

The people felt powerless, so they were acting out in the only way they knew how. Jude would give them their power back in the same way his father would have given it to them. "Let me ask you all something. Do you trust God?"

He could clearly hear some of the people saying 'no'. But with a louder voice others shouted 'Yes'. "Then let me tell you what we should do. We need to come together and pray; and then we need to protest." Jude held up a hand as he added, "Peaceably protest."

"Bring your signs, bring your heart for change, but most of all, bring your faith that if we all get together and march around this city demanding justice, that God will see to it that we get just what we pray for. Now are you with me?"

~~~~

"That's my boy," Isaac said as he watched the local news with Nina. "Do you see how he calmed that crowd and got them to follow him... born leader."

"Well, he is your son," Nina said.

"Tell him that I said to keep fighting the demonic forces that are trying to steal souls. Tell him to fight for me."

Nina glanced over at her husband. "What are you trying to say husband? You and I aren't done fighting, not by a long shot."

Isaac reached for Nina's hand. He gripped it as tight as he could. "I wish I could stay with you forever, Bae. Loving you has made this life worth living. I thank God every day that you gave me another chance after how I royally messed everything up for us."

She smiled at him as her mind drifted back in the day. "I never thought you and I would end up married and happy all these years like we've been, not when you were filled with so much rage and hatred to anything that opposed you."

"But God," Isaac said.

"But God, indeed," Nina responded. Because it had only been the grace of God that had saved Isaac and cleansed his heart in such a man that Nina truly believed her husband had received a heart transplant. Now she wondered if the time limit on that new heart was about to expire.

"I'm getting tired, Bae. Can you turn on my CD player? I want to listen to some praise music while I lay here?"

Nina went over to the CD player that she had brought into Isaac's hospital room because she knew how much he enjoyed gospel music. She opened the case of an old song that Isaac used to sing all the time when he first gave his life to the Lord. One time, she had even saw tears in her husband's eyes as he thought on the goodness of Jesus while singing Wonderful by Beau Williams. She put the CD in and walked back over to his bed.

The words, "Wonderful... God is so wonderful," bellowed from the small box and Isaac   started singing along... "Whatever I need the Lord will provide... and oh oh, you ought to try Him."

The music kept playing as Isaac grabbed hold of Nina's hand and told her, "Don't ever forget how much I have loved you."

"I won't, Isaac. I couldn't if I tried."

"Good... wonderful," he said and then drifted off to sleep.

~~~~

But this sleep was different. Isaac's eyes were still closed and he appeared to be sleep to anyone who might enter his room. But something was happening in the spirit realm. Isaac felt himself being pulled under and immediately knew he was about to enter the spiritual realm again. But there was no looming presence hawking over him, threatening to tear him from limb to limb. On the contrary. Isaac felt at peace, so he knew that the angel God had assigned to protect him for so many years must be nearby.

"You're here aren't you, old friend?"

As Brogan stepped forward a bright light shone in the room so devastating that Isaac lifted his arm above his eyes to shadow out some of the light. As the light diminished a vision of glory stood before him. Tall wouldn't be the right description because the angel was taller than any NBA player Isaac had ever seen. His wings were glorious and there was a mammoth size sword at his side. "I always knew I had an angel protecting me, but I never knew what you looked like."

"I am Brogan, and yes, I am here, Old Friend," Brogan told him as his voice quaked with emotion.

"Is it time?"

"Almost." Brogan held out a hand to Isaac as his wings flapped. "Come with me."

Isaac flung the covers off and eagerly followed the angel who had fought many battles for him throughout his lifetime. He didn't even question where they were going, because he trusted Brogan. What would be, would be because right now Isaac was safe in the arms of an angel. What a way to go.

As the journey ended and Isaac was standing on his own two feet, he watched in awe as beautiful pearl laden gates opened and music played... it sounded like a harp, but better than any harp Isaac had ever heard. He looked down and noticed that even though he didn't have on shoes, the ground beneath him was not hard or coarse. It was soft to the touch.

Angels stood outside the most magnificent pearl laden gates shouting, "Behold the Glory of God!"

Directly behind the pearly gates was a massive space where a cushion of snowy white clouds caressed the feet of its occupants. The tree of life stood bold and beautiful in the middle of the outer court. Its leaves were a heavenly green, and its fruit was succulent and enjoyed by all. Sweet blissful music could be heard throughout the great expanse of heaven.

There were thousands upon thousands of saints moving through the joys of heaven, clothed in glistening white robes, and bare feet. Many had crowns on their heads with various types of jewels embedded in them. Isaac shot a questioning glance at Brogan.

"These are the saints of God who have been washed in the blood of the Lamb. On Earth they walked that narrow path with God and they are now receiving their reward."

"And the people with jeweled crowns?" Isaac noted that some of the saints only had on white robes, but he took special note of the ones with the jeweled crowns. He needed to know if what he'd believed all these years was actually true."

"The jewels in the crown symbolize souls brought to Christ. There is actually many specs in each jewel that represent how many souls that saint brought to Christ."

"That's a blessing," Isaac said but as he looked at the people a little closer, he began noticing... he was pointing in the crowd, "Is that T-Bone?"

Brogan nodded. "He was the first person you led to Christ. He kept the faith until the day he died."

A woman named Marguerite Barrow stood, surrounded by the most beautiful array of flowers, colors without name. Heaven was the great garden of love, so these flowerbeds could be found all over this glorious place. As Marguerite stood in the midst of the splendor, the diamond in her crown sparkled brightly. She earned this diamond because of Nina, the girl she loved, sheltered and watered with the Word of the Lord. And Isaac remembered. He turned to Brogan. "That's the woman who brought Nina to Christ."

"Yes, Marguerite has enjoyed the peace and the joy of heaven for many years now".

Isaac was truly enjoying this trip to heaven as he was finally able to witness the end result of the work of the ministry. But then a young man walked up to him. He had on a white robe but no crown. He shook Isaac's hand.

"I'm Tony Jones, sir. I just wanted to thank you for making disciples because if you hadn't, Marissa wouldn't have reached out to me and I would never have accepted the Lord in my life."

As Tony walked back into the crowd of saints, Isaac felt tears rolling down his face. Isaac had expected to see this young man in the entrepreneur program at the church. But God had placed Tony in the ultimate program. The boy looked happy, filled with joy even.

To the right of this flowerbed stood a man with too many jewels for one crown to hold. For him, a glorious purple outer coat had also been made, and it glistened with the jewels of thousands of souls that had been won into the Kingdom.

Isaac's mouth hung open in astonishment. How could anyone have so many jewels that a coat of jewels had to be made for him?

Brogan told him, "On earth he had been a great pastor, one who believed in making disciples of God's people, rather than cripples. He didn't want his congregation to believe they could only find Jesus through him, but that they could find Him within their own hearts; and share Him with others. Because of this, many souls continued to be won into the Kingdom, even well after his death. His earthly congregation still remembers his teachings, and their eyes still mist at the thought of his great memory. His name was Willie E. Mitchell, Sr. He was the founder of Revival Center Ministries. He had been loved and respected by many, a modern day Job some might say. And now, as he walked in the midst of his friends, even as new jewels are added to his coat."

"He is still able to receive new jewels even after his death?"

"That's what happens when preachers make disciples. You will experience this yourself, my friend, because a coat is being made for you also. You did your job well Isaac, and your reward will be great in heaven."

15

"What do you mean, he won't wake up?" Jude was screaming at them. Donavan and Iona held onto his arm, trying to keep him from bursting into Isaac's room.

"The doctor said that his blood pressure dropped when he went to sleep and they haven't been able to wake him since," Donavan told him.

"So basically, my father is in a coma." Jude turned away from his family and punched the wall. "Why wasn't I here? Why did I listen to Mama and go out there to handle something the mayor could have found somebody else to do?"

"You were standing in for your dad, Jude. You did the right thing," Marissa tried to console him.

"Yeah well, now my dad is in a coma," Jude barked the words like a wounded lady animal.

"You need to calm down, little brother. Mama-Nina is in there with Dad, and we don't want to upset her any more than she already is," Iona told him.

"Aren't you upset? Are you afraid that this is it? That we'll never see Daddy again," Jude tore away from them and grabbed a chair in the waiting room and sat down. He closed his eyes as he took slow, deep breaths, trying to calm himself so he wouldn't put more on his mother than she could bear right now. But this was a heavy load for him too. How on earth was he going to get over something like this?

Jude had come straight from the March on City Hall to tell his father all that went down, how the people stopped rioting and looting and marched with him all through downtown declaring the name of the Lord and praying for justice.

"It's going to be alright, Jude." Marissa told him as she sat down next to him.

"How Marissa? How will this ever be okay?"

Tears fell from her eyes as she told him, "We have to trust God's plan. And you have to stay strong. God has something for you to do. I felt that so strongly as I stood with you today. Don't you feel it too?"

Her eyes implored him to rise up, and be the man she knew he could be. he wanted to be that man, but his dad wouldn't wake up and tell him what to do next. So, Jude felt stuck, like he had willed himself out of a fox hole, only to discover that the world had been nuked.

"Come on, Jude. Mama is going to need us," Donavan told him.

"It's not fair... It's not fair. Why did they have to birth me so late in life? Why didn't I realize that they were getting old?" Jude's hands went to his head as he lowered his head to his knees and moaned.

Marissa wrapped her arms around him real tight. "You can do this, Jude," she whispered in his ear. "I'm here with you. I'm not going nowhere, will get through this together, okay?"

She did it again. Her voice soothed him like no other could ever, would ever. Marissa was always supposed to be his, but he messed up. That was something he would have to live with for the rest of his life. But he was glad to have her with him tonight.

Jude took another deep breath, stood. He took hold of Marissa's hand and squeezed it. "I'm ready. Let's go see about Mama."

They opened the door to Isaac's hospital room, preparing themselves to see Nina tearfully falling apart beside her husband's bed, but that was not the case at all. Nina was on her knees, hands lifted and head raised heavenward, giving praise to God. "Lord, I thank You for all that You have done for me and Isaac. I thank You for the love You allowed us to share. I thank You for bringing Isaac Walker into my life and for making his heart big enough so that he was able to love You and love me as well.

"What a mighty God we serve… mighty, mighty, mighty God. You're wonderful in my sight… wonderful in Isaac's sight and I praise You that my husband has lived a long and fruitful life. I thank You for that because Isaac never thought he would live this long. Oh praise Your holy name."

She stood up and while clapping her hands Nina began roaming around the room as she continued to praise the Lord. But Jude put a hand on her shoulder, stopping her. "Is dad better or something?"

Nina was silent for a moment as she turned her head towards her husband. "He still hasn't woken up if that's what you mean."

"Is he just sleep or is something else going on?" Jude walked over to the bed and stared down at his father. His eye lids were closed but the eye balls beneath were moving back and forth as if his father was taking in sights that excited him. "If he's still alive, why won't he wake up?" Jude wanted to know.

"Only the Lord can answer that question," Nina told him.

Jude swung back around to face his mother. "Then why are you in here praising God as if everything is alright? Do you even care what is happening?"

"Don't attack Mama-Nina," Iona told him as she stepped toward Jude.

"I'm not attacking her. I just don't understand why she is in here praising God for my dad basically being in a coma."

"What else would you have me do? Yes, I want nothing more than to have my husband here with me. But if he is making his journey to paradise I can do nothing but praise the Lord for the man that your father is and for his finally getting the audience with the Lord that he most certainly deserves."

"You don't owe us an explanation, Mama. Whatever you want to do is fine with us," Donavan told Nina as he put an arm around her shoulder.

Jude shook his head. "I can't sit in here right now. I need to get some air." He swung open the door and stepped out of the room.

Marissa followed him. "Wait a minute, Jude." He stopped, waited on her to catch up. "Don't go off like this. Your mom needs all of you right now."

"This isn't a good time for me either, Marissa. But I'm not the one thanking God for taking my father from me." He pointed towards the door. "What in the world is she thinking?"

"She's trying not to be selfish, Jude. Can't you see that? She doesn't want to beg your father to stay here, if he is at rest and truly wants to be in heaven. I know that I wouldn't want to ask God to keep someone I loved here on earth if God is the One calling them home."

"Well, then you stay here with the rest of the praisers. I'm going to the chapel to tell God exactly what I think about this mess."

He left Marissa to go back into the room with his family while he went downstairs to the chapel. Jude sat down on the front bench and glared at the Jesus on the cross figure that was on the wall before him. Jude knew his Bible well. All of it had been spoon fed to him since he was born. Jesus had done his Father's will and carried his cross all the way to the place of his crucifixion. Jude knew that his father would want him to do exactly what his mother was in there doing. And then Isaac would expect him to go back out there tomorrow and continue leading that protest so that he could eventually lead souls to Christ. Jude also knew that was the right thing to do, because within months he had personally experienced the death of two men at the hand of the police. Stephen had never given his life to Christ and was now suffering in hell for that. But thanks to Marissa, Tony had discovered the love of God and Jude was confident that Tony was in heaven, rejoicing with the angels that his dad talked so much about.

Even so, this was a cross that Jude could not carry. He wasn't ready to say goodbye to his father. In the last few years Jude wouldn't have won any son of the year awards. He'd kept to himself as he dealt with the pain of losing Marissa and, yes, he could admit, as he moved further away from the Lord.

His eyes filled with unshed tears as he looked back toward the Jesus figure. "I don't want to live without him, Lord. Can't you understand that? I know that my father has been a good soldier in Your kingdom and all that. And I know that he might be tired and ready to go home to be with You, but I still need him."

"What you are doing is not right. When will you answer for all these lives that you just let drift away?" Jude yelled. He stayed in that spot and kept yelling at that Jesus figure on the wall for over an hour. Pointing out all his grievances. After that Jude was spent, he laid down on the bench, pulled his legs up to his chest and continued staring at the cross until his eyelids drooped. Jude then tried to get up, but he fell back against the bench and tried to get back up again, but couldn't as if some force was holding him there.

Then he heard a voice that was like the whirlwind saying, *"Who is this who request counsel by words without knowledge? Now prepare yourself like a man; I will question you, and you shall answer Me.*

Jude's eyes widened with fear. What was going on here? Who was speaking to him like this? Jude didn't have to wait long for his answer, because it soon became clear.

The Lord continued, *"Where were you, Judah, when I laid the foundations of the earth? Tell Me, if you have understanding. Who determined its measurements? Surely you know! Or who stretched the line upon it? To what were its foundations fastened? Or who laid its cornerstone? When the morning stars sang together, and all the sons of God shouted for joy? "Or who shut in the sea with doors, when it burst forth and issued from the womb? Who told the see, 'This far you may come, but no farther, and here your proud waves must stop!'*

"Have you commanded the morning since your days began, and caused the dawn to know its place, that it might take hold of the ends of the earth, and the wicked be shaken out of it?

Have the gates of death been revealed to you? Or have you seen the doors of the shadow of death?

Have you comprehended the breadth of the earth? Tell Me, if you know all this.

When the Lord was finished informing Judah of just who He really was, He said, *"Shall the one who contends with the Almighty correct Him?*

He who rebukes God, let him answer it."

~~~~

Isaac had been thoroughly enjoying himself in heaven with all of the witnesses for Christ gathered around giving praise to the Lord, "Glory to the Lamb that was slain and lives forever more."

But then in the next moment he was removed from the group of praising saints and taken into a smaller room. The floor of heaven opened and he was able to view Nina praising God for his entry into heaven. He smiled at that. He couldn't wait for his wife to join him, she would be so fascinated by the glory and beauty in the heavenly realm. But the smile was quickly removed from his face as he saw Jude railing against God and then he could see the whirlwind as he stood in front of his son and heard the angry voice of God as He schooled his wayward son.

Isaac fell on his knees. "Lord, My Lord, please forgive my son. He doesn't know... he doesn't understand. Jude has been through so much recently, he's hurting. Have mercy, Lord."

Brogan put a hand on Isaac's shoulder as he said, "He will be called Judah if he accepts the call of God on his life. But the time is short, he must choose."

Isaac turned to his old friend. He implored Brogan, "You can help him. Go to Judah, and be with him as you were with me."

"Judah is my next assignment. But he will need your help as well if he is to accept the call of God on his life."

"What do you mean? How can I help him now?"

"It is up to Judah. If he accepts God's call, then he will need you to guide him into the next level of the vision God gave you."

"So, you're saying that Judah was always meant to take the ministry to the next level? And all those obstacles that got in my way, were from God?"

Brogan nodded. Then he turned Isaac's hands over so that he could see that they were dripping with blood.

"Why?" Isaac was confused. Why would his hands be dripping with blood while in heaven.

"Once you make your final entry into heaven you will be totally washed by the blood of the Lamb. But while on earth you still have the blood of all the people you murdered on your hands. This is why you cannot carry the ministry to the next level… but Judah can. He was born to further your ministry on the earth."

"What if he doesn't accept?"

"Then there is no need for you to go back. You will stay here and I suppose I will be assigned to someone else."

Isaac got back on his knees and kept praying.

~~~~

Meanwhile Jude's eyes were wild as he tried to gird himself in order to answer the Lord. His father had this spiritual gift of being able to see within the spiritual realm and somehow, Jude was now able to do the same. So far though he'd only been taking horrid trips to hell and back. He'd never had an audience with the Lord, but he'd never spoken so disrespectfully to the Lord either.

He lowered his head and cried like he was a new born baby that had just had his bottom spanked. "How can I answer you Lord? I should do nothing but put my hand over my mouth because I have no right to even be speaking to You. I have no answer for my behavior. I am a man ashamed of the way I have lived my life." And that was the truth, for no matter what Jude had done in the years since college, he had one great desire, which was to make his father proud. And he knew that the way he had been living had not been anything to be proud of.

Then the Lord answered Judah out of the whirlwind, and said: "Would you indeed annul My judgment? Would you condemn Me that you may be justified? Have you an arm like God? Or can you thunder with a voice like Mine?

"Then adorn yourself with majesty and splendor, And array yourself with glory and beauty. Disperse the rage of your wrath; Look on everyone who is proud, and bring him low; Tread down the wicked in their place. Hide them in the dust together, Bind their faces in hidden darkness. If you can do any of that, then *I will also confess to you, that your own right hand can save you."*

Holding his hand against his head, Jude acknowledged, "Cannot save myself. I need You, Lord just like anyone else. I shouldn't have spoken. It is up to You, Lord to do what You will with my father. I will accept Your will."

16

"Can I talk to you for a minute, Mama," Jude asked as he opened the door to his father's hospital room.

Nina was holding onto Isaac's hand as she reclined in the recliner next to Isaac's bed. She sat up, still holding onto her husband's hand she turned to the others in the room and said, "Can you all give Jude and I a moment?"

Keith and Cynda were in the room now. They got up just as Iona, Marissa and Donavan did and walked out of the room.

Jude sat down in the chair next to Nina. He didn't say anything for a minute as he stared at Isaac laying there so still, so quiet. Jude had never known his father to be quiet or still a moment in his life. It was hard for him to see him like this, knowing that he couldn't just shake his shoulder and wake him up.

"Doesn't this whole thing make you sad? Am I so wrong to want my father to stay with us a little longer?"

"You're not wrong at all, hon. I want him to stay with us also. I plan to stay right here holding onto his hand until I'm told that I have to let him go."

"I don't know what to do, Mama. I'm supposed to be at a rally tomorrow but I'm terrified that while I'm there trying to help other people, my father might die while I'm gone. How can I live with that?"

Nina rubbed Isaac's hand as she said, "Before your father went to sleep-"

"Why do you keep saying he's asleep? If he can't wake himself up then he must be in a coma, right?"

Sighing, Nina said, "If your father is right now transitioning then I call it a sleep. Because when we are in Christ we never truly die. We may put aside our earthly body but the spirit will live forever."

"I believe that too," Jude admitted. "I couldn't grow up in the Walker household and not believe it. I'm not trying to question God," Jude tried to make clear before he continued, "but I just don't know why God would take Dad when he still has so much work to do."

"Your father told me to tell you something before he fell asleep. He said that you should keep fighting the demonic forces that are trying to steal souls."

"He said that?"

Nina nodded. "He also asked that you fight for him."

"He's the demon slayer, not me."

"I think you have forgotten who you really are, Isaac Judah Walker. I've always known that God had some kind of special ministry for you. I've already apologized to your father and now I will apologize to you, because I now realize that you were never meant to go off to college. I truly believe that you were supposed to stay right here and continue the evangelistic ministry Isaac began with those street revivals."

"I loved being in college. I'm glad that you changed my mind about going."

"It was a good thing to do, but was it the right thing for you? Search your heart, Jude. Ask God to show you what He wants from you."

Jude didn't know if he wanted to question God again anytime soon. He'd rather his father woke up and told him what he should do next. He got out of his seat and walked over to Isaac's bed. Looking down at his father, Jude felt tears in his eyes. He quickly wiped them away because he knew his mother wouldn't like that.

His father lived his life fighting for people who didn't know how to fight for themselves. Isaac Walker had been through so much and survived it all. Isaac Walker had always been a force to be reckoned with. People didn't give him trouble on the streets, because Isaac had man handled the streets when he had been running drugs back in the day.

Jude didn't know much about the streets, when he'd been seventeen he tried to be a gang banger and figured out real quick that he wasn't cut out for that lifestyle. Looking back at his mom with anguish etched in his face, Jude told her, "I can't be like him. I may look like him, but we are two totally different people... with different life experiences."

Nina gently released Isaac's hand, stood up and walked over to her son. She turned him to face her as she said, "I never correct anyone who calls you junior, because you do have your father's first name. But do you know why I gave you a middle name, even though your father doesn't have one?"

"Because you wanted me to always remember to praise the Lord," Jude said in a sing-songy way as if he had heard it all before.

"That was one reason. But I also did it so you'd remember that you aren't Isaac Walker. There will only ever be one like my man. But you are Isaac Judah Walker, and there will only ever be one like you."

The door opened, Donavan poked his head in. "Jude, I just wanted to let you know that I'm going to give Marissa a ride home."

"That's a good idea," Nina said, "All of y'all should go home and get some rest."

"But what about Daddy?" Jude was terrified that the moment he left, he would receive a call telling that his dad passed away.

"Your daddy ain't going no where. He is going to wait right here so I can tell him how many lives were shook up by your march on City Hall tomorrow."

~~~~

Jude was wore out from his encounter with God so he took his mom's advice and went to her house so he could get some sleep. But he still wasn't sure if he was going to lead that march in the morning. Who did he think he was anyway? He was just a guy who started off wanting to bring souls to Christ, who sold out so that his app could make more money and make him rich. So, how could he reach people and bring them to the Lord like his parents want him to do, when he felt so utterly lost himself?

He went upstairs, jumped in the shower, then went to his old bedroom, put on a pair of pj's and flopped into the bed head first. Jude was drifting off to sleep when suddenly he felt something grabbing and pulling on him. Immediately, he knew what was happening and he tried to break free and not let the demons win... he did not want to be drug into Hades not one more time in life. "Please no," he screamed.

But it was no use, Jude's eyes opened in a room that was red from all the blood dripping off the walls. Jude put his hands to his ears because screeching screaming noises were coming from those bloody walls. "Help me... help me... help me" He kept hearing those words over and over. But how could he help? He couldn't even see the people behind that wall.

Then one by one faces started appearing all around the room. He'd seen some of those people out rioting and looting yesterday. Jude didn't know why the faces were so familiar to him, but as each face flashed before him he could recall where he'd seen this or that person. The one yelling for help right now, he remembered seeing as he threw a rock into the window of a department store. The next face he saw in the bloody wall was that of a woman he'd seen running out of that department store with an arm full of stolen clothes.

He saw the faces of so many people he had the opportunity to minister to through out the years but Jude had ignored them. "These people aren't dead." Jude shook his head as if the display before him was just shameful.

But then a monstrous demon slithered toward him, hissing and laughing at him. "They'll be here soon enough. Because we stopped you from figuring it out."

"Figure what out?"

The demon disappeared and Jude was left screaming until his screams shook him out of yet another nightmare. He was now woke, but still not comforted because he was being tormented by the fact that he obviously missed something. He had a feeling that figuring out this next journey of his life could possibly mean everything to so many people.

Images of him at numerous street revivals with his father flashed through his head. Jude felt relaxed and at peace as one image after the next of women and men walking to the altar to give their lives to the Lord sped by him. But the one image that seemed to slow down was of Marissa walking towards the altar.

As she lifted her hands and accepted Jesus Christ into her life, Jude this monstrous beat float out of her body and the name of that beast was Death. Jude watched Death slither away looking for another body to climb into, but as Isaac kept preaching and proclaiming the name of the Lord, Death couldn't find a body at the revival and was forced to leave their presence.

He sat up in bed wondering what in the world had God just revealed to him. Then Jude remembered a comment by Marissa from many years ago. He had said that he wished he had met her after the drama with Calvin Jones, because then she never would have gotten hurt and lost her baby.

But Marissa had told him that if he hadn't knocked on her door that day, then they probably never would have met. Did she know that she was scheduled to die? How did she know? Then suddenly it all seemed clear to Jude. Marissa had planned to kill herself. God planned for Jude to knock on her door at the exact moment he'd done so. He had been sent there to save her life and then his father preached the message that allowed Marissa to accept God into her life so that her soul could be saved.

Coming to the realization that ministry mattered, and that it not only changed lives but saved them, was all too overwhelming for him. Because Jude was finally accepting the truth. That the years he spent only being concerned with making money and not the cause of Christ has consequences. Somebody out there needed him to knock on their door... needed him to tell them about a God who is quick to save. But Jude had failed. He put his hands to his head and bowed low as he yelled out into the atmosphere, "Who am I? Why am I here? What did I miss and how did I miss it?"

Once again Jude heard the still small voice coming to him out of a whirlwind. *"You are Judah, you were born to give me praise. Walk upright before Me."*

He got out of his bed and bowed down on his knees, lifted up his hands like he hadn't done in years. "Forgive me Lord, I was wrong. I didn't understand." Tears were streaming down his face as he said, "I want to be used by You. Show me where to go... tell me what to do. But most of all, don't ever take your spirit away from me. Jesus, I promise, if You restore my soul, I'll never turn away from You again."

17

The moment his eyes opened that morning, he picked up the phone and called the hospital. Once he got his mother on the phone he asked, "How is Dad doing?"

"There's no change. He is still asleep."

His mother would not say the word 'coma'. She just kept saying he was resting or sleep. Yesterday such talk ticked him off, but this morning it only put a smile on his face, because he now saw those words as her faith in action. "I have to go to the rally this morning. But I will be at the hospital the moment I'm done."

"That's fine, Jude. And I want you to know that you're father would be proud of you for doing this."

"I know he would… and Mama, please call me Judah from now on. I'm ready to be the man I was supposed to be from the moment I was born."

"Thank you, Jesus," Nina said in a low voice as if she was trying not to disturb Isaac.

"Pray for me, Mama because I don't want to turn my back on my destiny ever again."

"I will pray, son. Now you go do what your father told you."

Judah left the house confident in what he was to do for the day, but he still had many questions. God had restored him and wanted him in the ministry, that much was clear to Judah, but he wasn't quiet sure what his next move should be. How was he supposed to start his ministry? So many questions that Judah wished he could sit at his dad's feet and soak up all the knowledge that man had. He took a deep breath as he got out of his car and met up with the hundreds of people that were waiting for them to begin their march to City Hall. "One day at a time... one step at a time," he told himself as they began the march.

Several pastors had joined the march today, so when they reached the destination each of them took turns speaking. When it was Judah's turn he held onto the mic for a moment. Not saying anything but silently praying for God to direct him. He cleared his throat and said, "My name is Judah Walker, and I'm so thankful for the preachers who came out today and admonished us all to keep the faith even in these troubling times.

"But I also understand there are many of you who are having trouble with all this stuff we are seeing, sometimes on a daily basis. So, I'm the last one to tell you to just believe and everything will turn out all right. Because you see, I lost my faith several years ago and I'm just now getting it back.

"All I can tell you all is that I thought I didn't need God. I thought I would be just fine in this world because I was making money and living good. But when things started to fall apart, and I didn't have my faith to fall back on, I fell apart.

"We have a right to be angry. And we have a right to stand up for what is right, but to lose hope and give up your faith, that would be like bringing about another death... a spiritual one that many people never recover from."

When Judah finished speaking he did something that he often saw his father do... he made an altar call. As dozens of men and women came forward to accept the Lord Jesus Christ into their lives Judah and the other preachers prayed with them. Judah smiled as he saw Marissa for the first time that day. He didn't know she was at the rally until she took the spot next to him and began praying for a woman as she cried in Marissa's arms... ministry.

When they were finished, Judah slid his hand in Marissa's as they walked back to their cars. "Thanks for coming out here today."

"I wouldn't have missed it." Marissa smiled up at him as she added, "Looks like someone spent a little extra time with God last night."

"I figured some things out," he told her, grinning.

"Do you want to talk about it?"

He stopped walking, still holding on to her hand and looked her in the eye. "I want to ask you about something. This might be a little awkward, but I need to know." She nodded, giving him the go ahead. "Were you planning to kill yourself the day I knocked on your door?"

Marissa stepped back from Judah and put a hand over her mouth. "How did you know that?"

"Seriously, if I told you, I don't even think you'd believe me. Let me just say that I dreamed about the day you gave your life to the Lord last night. And I saw something in the spirit that I didn't notice that day."

"God is really using you, Jude."

"I'm Judah now," he corrected.

"I heard you say Judah when you introduced yourself to the crowd. God is doing a work in you." She hugged him.

Emotions flowed through Judah that he couldn't control. He loved this woman, but he didn't want to overwhelm her with everything he was dealing with.

"What's wrong?" Marissa asked him.

He hesitated a moment, but then just as he opened his mouth to respond, his phone beeped. He glanced at the text message. It said, 'We need you at the hospital'. Judah's eyes widened.

Marissa asked again, "What's wrong?"

Judah's voice broke as he said, "They need me at the hospital."

"Let me drive you there, Judah. I don't think you should be alone right now."

He wanted to man up and tell her that he could handle it. But in truth, Judah didn't know if he could handle this moment alone. He had made the right decision to come out here and speak life to these people... he would always remember the looks on some of the faces as they accepted Christ. But if his father passed away before he got to the hospital, Judah didn't know how he would feel about that. "Thank you for being here with me, Marissa. God knows I need you right now."

He let her drive him to the hospital. They were quiet on the drive over, neither expressing their thoughts. Neither wanting to declare that this just might be the end. But one thing Judah knew for sure... he wasn't suffering alone, because Isaac Walker wasn't just his father, but he was also the closest thing to a father Marissa had ever known.

He glanced over at her and saw a few tears rolling down her face. "Do you need to pull over so I can drive?"

"You just sit over in that passenger seat and mind your own business. I'm supposed to be helping you right now."

"It's not going to be very helpful if you run us into a ditch because you're blinded by tears. So, just pull over and I'll drive us."

Marissa wiped the tears from her face and then said, "What tears? You think you know so much, but you don't know everything, Mr. Judah."

His phone beeped again. Judah looked at it. This text was from Iona. It said, "What's taking you so long... you're missing out."

He texted back. "Missing out on what?"

Judah told Marissa about the text and then asked, "What do you think she means by that? Do you think the doctor told them that he's getting ready to go any minute or something?"

"I don't know Judah. Let's just pray that we make it in time, okay?"

And so they prayed.

~~~~

Marissa and Judah sprinted through the hospital. Judah hit the elevator button like it owed him money. And then they fidgeted while waiting the full three seconds for the elevator to arrive. But once they were standing in front of Isaac's hospital room, Marissa put a hand on the door, but Judah stopped her.

When she gave him a quizzical glance, he said, "I need you to pray that no matter what I encounter in that room, it won't stop me from fulfilling everything God has for me."

But she told him. "When you caught me crying, it wasn't for Pastor Isaac because I know he's going to be alright no matter what. But I was silently crying out to God for you and your ministry."

Judah couldn't help himself, this was the woman God had for him from the moment they met. He had messed up and let her get away, but he wasn't about to let her go now. He leaned forward and kissed her and Marissa kissed him right back. "I love you," he whispered in her ear and then opened the door to his father's room, confident that he would be able to handle what came next.

But Judah almost passed out when he saw his father sitting up in bed with a fork and knife in his hand as he cut the steak he was chowing down on.

Isaac looked up and grinned at him as he shouted, "I'm back boy. We've got work to do."

"What? Huh?" Judah turned to his mother. "How long has he been woke?"

Nina stood, walked over to Judah and gave him the biggest hug he'd ever received from her. "He woke up about an hour ago. He told me he watched your altar call from heaven… and that your accepting the call of God on your life is the only reason he is here with us."

Judah was stunned. He glanced around the room to see all the family who'd squeezed in… everybody was grinning from ear to ear. Isaac was back and Judah was happy as well, but he was confused.

Isaac pushed his plate aside and called Judah closer. "Son, you received the gift of being able to see into the spiritual realm from me. That knowledge terrified me, because I know how many times your dreams will be haunted with monstrous beasts trying to claw your eyes out. But I'm praying that one day, the good Lord will also allow you a glimpse of

Heaven… and Judah, I promise you, it will be all worth it."

"So, you've been to Heaven?"

Isaac nodded.

Then Judah said, "I always thought that if a man entered into Heaven then he'd never want to come back to earth."

Isaac put Nina's hand in his. He kissed his wife, but then told Judah, "I'm not here for myself. I doubt if I will live long enough to see the full manifestation of all God has in store for you, but I'm here to help you build your ministry for as long as God allows."

Nina interjected, "I'm not ever going to get in the way of God's business again, but I hope you'll find the time give me and your father some grandkids while we're still able to see and hold them."

Isaac giggled at his wife, but Judah didn't think anything was funny. He was stone cold serious as he turned to Marissa and said, "What do you think, Bae? I know you don't want to disappoint my mom."

Marissa's eyebrow's arched as she put a hand on her hips. "Just when am I supposed to be having all these kids for you."

He took her in his arms, not caring about all the eyes that were on them. "About two seconds after I make you my wife."

"So, you think you're going to marry me, huh?"

"Think I'm not," he told her as he lowered his head and kissed her with all the hunger that had been locked in inside of him for years. Marissa was always destined to be his, but Judah had not been worthy of her until this very moment. He would thank the Lord for the rest of his life for bringing Marissa back into his life.

When their lips parted, Marissa stumbled backward. Grabbed hold of the chair behind her and then asked, "Do I at least get a ring?"

The room erupted in laughter... because after all, laughter was good like a medicine.

Epilogue

Marissa was a June bride and all their family and friends were there to see the beautiful and blessed union of Isaac Judah Walker and Marissa Walker. Within the space of five years, Judah's street ministry grew to the point where he was having to rent out football stadiums to hold his events. The ministry wasn't the only thing that had grown. Because Marissa had given birth to two handsome little boys and one beautiful little girl.

The girl had been born exactly five years after Isaac opened his eyes in the very same hospital that Marissa delivered the newest addition to the family. And it was on that day, as Isaac sat down in the rocking chair in the family birthing room and held his granddaughter in his arms that he closed his eyes and eternally slept with his Heavenly Father.

Nina's heart didn't survive long without Isaac and within a year she joined her husband in the land where streets were paved in gold and flowers were ever blooming. When she approached her earthly husband, Nina couldn't help but smile because Isaac was now wearing the exact same coat that had been adorned with the many jewels that he had admired on another pastor when he first visited Heaven. Her husband had received his reward and now she was about to receive hers. "Great is the Lord and worthy is He to be praised," Isaac shouted as he saw her approaching.

"What a mighty God we have served," she answered back. And the cloud of witnesses gathered around and they all began to praise the Lord for the good things He has done. No more rain would be coming Isaac's and Nina's way, only sunshine from here on out.

The End

To join my mailing list:
http://vanessamiller.com/events/join-mailing-list/
Join me on Facebook: https://www.facebook.com/groups/77899021863/
Join me on Twitter: https://www.twitter.com/vanessamiller01

Books in the RAIN series

Former Rain (Book 1)

Abundant Rain (Book 2)

Latter Rain (Book 3)

Rain Storm (Book 4)

Through the Storm (Book 5)

Rain For Christmas (Book 6)

After the Rain (Book 7)

Rain in the Promised, Land (Book 8)

About the Author

Vanessa Miller is a best-selling author, playwright, and motivational speaker. She started writing as a child, spending countless hours either reading or writing poetry, short stories, stage plays and novels. Vanessa's creative endeavors took on new meaning in1994 when she became a Christian. Since then, her writing has been centered on themes of redemption, often focusing on characters facing multi-dimensional struggles.

Vanessa's novels have received rave reviews, with several appearing on *Essence Magazine's* Bestseller's List. Miller's work has receiving numerous awards, including "Best Christian Fiction Mahogany Award" and the "Red Rose Award for Excellence in Christian Fiction." Miller graduated from Capital University with a degree in Organizational Communication. She is an ordained minister in her church, explaining, "God has called me to minister to readers and to help them rediscover their place with the Lord."

She has worked with numerous publishers: Urban Christian, Kimani Romance, Abingdon Press and Whitaker House. She is currently indy published through Praise Unlimited enterprises and working on the Family Business Series.

In 2016, Vanessa launched the Christian Book Lover's Retreat in an effort to bring readers and authors of Christian fiction together in an environment that's all about Faith, Fun & Fellowship. To learn more about Vanessa, please visit her website: www.vanessamiller.com. If you would like to know more about the Christian Book Lover's Retreat that is currently held in Charlotte, NC during the last week in October you can visit: http://www.christianbookloversretreat.com/index.html

Don't forget to join my mailing list:
http://vanessamiller.com/events/join-mailing-list/
Join me on Facebook: https://www.facebook.com/groups/77899021863/
Join me on Twitter: https://www.twitter.com/vanessamiller01

CPSIA information can be obtained
at www.ICGtesting.com
Printed in the USA
LVOW13s1618231216
518585LV00009B/291/P